This book is dedicated to young people everywhere.

The Story of Sirio

Ferdinando Camon

The Story of Sirio

A Parable

Translated from the Italian by
Cassandra Bertea

THE MARLBORO PRESS

T M P

MARLBORO, VERMONT

1985

Originally published in Italian as
STORIA DI SIRIO
© Aldo Garzanti Editore, 1984.

Manufactured in the United States of America.

Library of Congress Catalog Card Number 84-63123

ISBN 0-910395-12-8

CONTENTS

The Story of Sirio

PART ONE: THE CAREER

1: ON TOP OF THE CITY

Sirio was the son of an important manufacturer and he lived with his family in the residential tower in the center of town. Every evening, while the servants were preparing to serve supper in the dining room, his father would step out with him onto the terrace and have him look at the city at that moment when its lights came on.

A little before sundown the city seemed to disappear: invading fog would start to move in from the horizon, first enwrapping the suburbs (formerly outlying villages, then engulfed by the city as it expanded out upon the plain, like a great stain that as it spreads over the table absorbs the crumbs) and then slipping in along the main avenues which seen from above resembled broad rivers furrowing the uniform surface of constructions, and from there the clouds of fog headed for the heart of the city. Seen from high up the city seemed mute: busses appeared to move slowly, like pachyderms in the jungle, and cars swarmed in every direction, but not the least sound was to be heard: as if every motor was switched off.

When the fog had invaded the central square too, burying the cathedral and the rows of arcades adjoining it, you could say the whole city had vanished: from the tower nothing remained visible except the tower itself rising from the rolling banks of fog, just as the look-out of a sinking vessel sees nothing except the mast he is perched upon.

Against the corners of the tall building a continuous wind hissed day and night, summer and winter, and this was the only sound that might have been heard had not one's ears got used to it and by now become incapable of distinguishing it, mistaking that sound for silence. The reinforced concrete tower was flexible and when occasional gusts struck its upper stories, the summit of the skyscraper would sway ever so slightly, too imperceptible for anyone to notice save perhaps as a vague feeling of dizziness.

In Sirio's home most of the time is spent sitting down. At table, in front of the television set, or in easy chairs with visiting friends; or every evening at sunset, on the terrace looking out over the disappearing and reappearing city.

The instant after the sun goes down lights suddenly go on all over the city, and then you see whole neighborhoods showing through seams in the fog, and streets flanked by rows of streetlights stand out straight as runways at an airport. Sirio had flown a few times, with his father, to New York, to London and to Paris, and he remembered that the runways are lit by two rows of light from very early evening until well after sunrise, and that the plane, as soon as it touches down, rushes between those lines of light as if between two lanes of fire.

And so from the top of the tower the city appears when its lights suddenly go on: looking at it from up there you can make everything out as if upon a map. But to make everything even easier, out on the terrace, upon a special stand, there is indeed a relief map so positioned as to seem exactly superimposed upon the city. And the map lights up too, at sundown, and when lit various colors shine up from it; the zones that belong entirely or in large part to the Company are red or orange, those that are to some lesser extent under its control are pink, all the others white. There is a button below the map and next to the button are the words: *You are here:* touch the button and a little red dot blinks on the map, and that's the spot where you are.

Next to the red button there is an entire battery of buttons, each marked: Management, Plant, Research and Development, Testing Facilities, Warehousing, and Sales. These are the different divisions that compose the Automobile Manufacturing Corporation that Sirio's family owns. Pushing all the buttons you discover that the Company occupies not just a section of the city but is spread out a bit everywhere: as if the various divisions also had the function of dominating the city, overseeing it, holding it in custody. Below the keyboard is a list of streets: they are the streets where the Company owns some major piece of property, a distinguished building, a bank, a clinic; each street is identified by a number and if you press that number, the corresponding street lights up on the map. Press all the buttons and all the numbers on the luminous map and practically the whole city comes alight: in appearance it is now an extension of the Great Factory, an artificial appendage to it, so to speak.

All this is why every evening father and son wait for the lights of the city to come on: they all but have the impression that God himself illuminates the map of their possessions.

Manipulating buttons and numbers, they do indeed have the feeling of the city lying in their hands.

From up there father and son gaze at it for an instant, trying to determine to where, as of tonight, the lights have advanced, and remarking to one another:

"You can even see the hills."

"You can even see the sea."

Before going back inside, the father places a hand on his son's shoulder and stretches out his other hand, gesturing towards sectors not yet conquered.

"Tomorrow, my boy, your task will be to reach all the way out to there."

The son looks at the illuminated city—white and purple—then extends his hands over the map and pushes buttons at random: red, orange, pink, white. Silently he looks at that expanse of light, buildings, churches, hospitals, and within himself he has no doubt: his purpose in life, the meaning of his life is to take command of all this, increase it, and transmit it in his turn to the son he will have one day.

2: Having a Job

Some mornings Sirio would go to the factory by car with his father, and then it seemed that his father was at his disposal, ready to show him the offices, the machines, the products. If Sirio expressed a wish or asked a question, his father would be at pains to grant it at once or to provide an answer, even if to do so meant changing his plans for that morning. When he was a small boy Sirio had asked simple questions, of the kind: "Do robots talk?" In the car his father used to laugh; the driver never laughed. His father would reply right away: "Today you shall see the robots." As soon as they reached the factory Sirio's father would call in his secretary and tell her he wanted to speak to the head of the Robot Team. The secretary would go back to her office and would call Workers Management on the interphone, informing them that the boss wanted the head of the Robot Team. And Workers Management would call Robot Management. Robot

Management would get hold of the foreman in charge of the Robot Team, telling him to come right over.

The order had now to be executed, that is, the Robot Team foreman had to betake himself all the way up to the boss's level. To accomplish this, at the factory there existed a mechanism that strongly reminded one of the locks in the Panama Canal. In Panama it is also a matter of raising something—a vessel—and conveying it from a lower ocean to a higher ocean. To this end the canal is divided into several closed compartments and in each compartment the vessel is raised a little. At the factory it is the same thing: when something—a subordinate—is to be raised to the boss's level, the distance separating that subordinate from the boss is divided into so many segments, and the subordinate proceeds through these one at a time, as if they were legs in a journey, and with each leg he mounts a little higher. To begin with, the subordinate breaks off from his work and proceeds to his department supervisor's office. Here they remove his card from the board—he is no longer on the job—they promptly designate his replacement from the reserve pool, and they direct him to the Management Office upstairs. Here they advise him that General Management has called for him. At General Management they explain to him that he has been called for by the boss and must therefore present himself to his secretary. In the secretary's office his progress comes to an end, for he is not a ship that must traverse the entire canal and proceed on into the other ocean: once got this far, they explain to him that he is to go back down with the boss's son, for whom he is henceforward responsible, and show him the robots at work. The Robot Team foreman makes no vocal response—his voice might carry beyond the forbidden threshold and

reach the other side—but nods, nods also to the boss's
son, heads back with him, follows the corridor back to the
elevator, goes back down to his department, goes toward
the Robot Team. All along the way all those who see him
in the company of the boss's son look first at the son and
then at him, then look again, as if to convince themselves
that yes, they have actually entered into contact, these
two points, the one so high, the other so low.

The Robot Team is a team of welders. The robots are
chunkily built, compact, but not small, with pincers for
hands and for feet a pair of skis that slide forward and
backward within grooves. When the part to be welded
approaches the robot's station the robot starts forward.
Once the part is blocked in position the robot bends and
touches it with its two pincers. The pincers sparkle and
the metal is welded. The robot lets go of the part,
straightens up, retreats to its waiting position. Released,
the welded part is snatched up, it hangs in the air by a
wire, it sways: swaying, off it moves while behind it the
robot bends brightly over the next part that is already
there waiting.

Watching the robot's performance, Sirio was filled with
amazement: for it was the vision of a man created by man.

Seeing the boss's son so happy, the Robot Team foreman thought to make him even happier: as the robot was
advancing towards a part to be welded he stepped
forward and cut in front of it. The robot saw him, came to
an abrupt halt with a fluttering of its hands and, brought
thus to a standstill, turned its head—perfectly spheri-
cal—to the right and to the left in sign of perplexity. But
by now the space in front of it had been cleared and the
robot was skiing forward once again, bending over the
part to be welded, sparkling. Sirio wondered where the

9

robot's eyes were and at the same time told himself that the day robots filled the factory happiness would reign at last.

But just as it already was the factory seemed happy to him, and Sirio knew that the aim in life of many of his contemporaries was to be able to work at the factory: to have a job.

Sirio had a friend whose name was Cino. Cino often came to the factory with him, or came to his house to play with the luminous map, or went with him for a stroll around the factory divisions. Cino was lucky because he was the son of the General Manager and the friend of the owner's son: tomorrow he too would become General Manager: therein lay the meaning of his life, for him it could have no other.

And thus were the lives of Sirio, of Cino and of all the youngsters of their age interwoven one with the other: Sirio would be the boss, Cino would be the General Manager and all the others would be administrators, employees, workers. Sirio's future gave meaning to the future of all the others and vice versa. The future that Sirio sensed to be his was something that concerned not only himself or his friends or his family, it concerned the system.

In the factory there was a spot that came to be called "The Observatory" because from there you could see the termination of the assembly line: the by now completed cars, finished, perfect, ready to be tested. The last part to be added was the factory trade mark. This medallion was placed, at the front, on the radiator cowl; at the rear, on the lid of the baggage compartment. The workers who put this final part on—simple pressure of the fingers sufficed to make it slip into place—would take advantage of the closeness of the finished car to stroke its flanks, run a

hand over its windows, open and shut a door, wipe the
dashboard. Not one of them would ever own that model
but they all had the first minute of every car, and by the
end of the day each had had his fill, as if he had put in
thousands of kilometers behind the wheel.

The Observatory was a balcony on the top floor and
from there you could see in addition to the finished products coming off the main assembly line those others that
were custom-built. The latter were all different from one
another, each born from a customer's particular taste and
answering to his particular needs: one wanted a very long
and stately vehicle, one an aerodynamic sports car, one
wanted his car comfortable and luxurious. Each, when he
ordered, specified measurements and color scheme and
furnished complete drawings. Each of these special re-
quests would be examined and studied, and if it was of
outstanding interest it would even come under discussion
and be kept on file in the Technical Bureaus.

From up upon the Observatory you could see the custom-built cars arrive at the last stage of the assembly line
and come off it completed, bright-colored and brand new.
Looking at them you had a panorama of people's tastes:
into the product that they had desired, planned, waited
years for, the customers had poured their personal fan-
cies, their own sense of beauty, of life, their own dreams.
He who governs should know what his subjects dream
about.

The factory was located on the edge of the city in what
once had been a village and was now, owing to the city's
growth, turned into a suburb. The city advances through
the villages of the plain with the effect of a magnet amidst
iron filings: the filings stir, shift direction, are attracted,
adhere. Likewise the villages: they swell in the valleys,

lengthen along the roads, grow towards the city until they fasten on to it. After that they do not let go. For so many years now has happiness coincided with being in the city, and the right to happiness is the right to the city. The lives human beings are leading divide into two great sorts: those that unfold in the city and that are lived by people who think continually about themselves, and those that unfold outside, where people think continually about the city. The factory is the means and the place for obtaining both these rights: the right to happiness and the right to the city. Therefore it may be further said that the right men aspire to in order to give meaning to their lives is the right to a job. That is why the factory stands at the threshold to the city. Beyond the factory begins the countryside.

A few steps into the countryside and there are the testing grounds. Here all the cars the factory produces are tried out. The grounds have several circuits, with cars of the same horsepower being run on each. The drivers who test the cars wear white overalls; on their breast pocket they wear the same trade mark that is on the car, and this tells you right away that the Company does its testing here. Every circuit is at all times full of cars, all being driven at the same speed. And the spectacle of this uniformity is a sign of the uniformity towards which life tends: they who purchase the cars will go at the same speed, will meet with the same maintenance costs, will have the same breakdowns; in a word, the acquiring of the same model unifies their lives much more than does marriage.

When his father had a little spare time he would invite Sirio and Cino for a complete tour. First of all he would take them up to the Observatory and from there would

point out to them what was coming off the various assembly lines, and would explain why from among many
projects the Company had settled upon these particular
ones, with this style, that amount of power, those per-
formances. Thus Sirio learned that there was a relationship between the nation's level of prosperity and the
models put out by the Company, between the price of
utility compacts and the rise in the number of marriages,
between the performance of small cars for women and
women's autonomy in society.

From the Observatory his father would accompany
him, when he was by himself, to the Technical Bureaus
and show him the top-secret plans that no one could
know about and that concerned cars the Company would
be bringing out within one, two or three years. On paper
these projects were only figures, sketches, drawings, studies. But there was a place where these seemed like real
cars, and this was at Body Testing: here wax or plastic
replicas of the models stood upon a turntable, and around
this table the design engineers sat in silence, gazing at
them, and smoking. Every once in a while someone
would get up, go over to one of the mock-ups and alter a
detail. What amazed Sirio was the discovery that each of
these designers was endeavoring to visualize the model
through the eyes of the public and in proposing changes
was adjusting it closer, not to an ideal of his own, but to
that of the future buyers: each designer was experiencing
now emotions and reactions that the public would experience in the years to come. In that department, essentially,
they were living life years in advance.

Then his father would accompany Sirio to the little
hilltop overlooking the circuits. Here his father would
stop talking: for half an hour he'd watch the cars roaring

around the tracks and wouldn't say a word. Sirio would look at the tracks swarming with cars: the result, colorful and functioning, of the labor of thousands of persons buried in the factory shops; he'd look at his silent father; he'd look at the surrounding hills; and he'd think that some day he too would have the feeling of producing new models, of experiencing in advance the emotions people were going to have, of allowing a fresh contingent of humankind to realize its right to the city.

At his side Cino had more or less the same thoughts: he would be the Manager of the thousands of persons whose labor produced these results, he'd be privy to the boss's plans and would translate them into reality.

This was what life meant, and of this Sirio and Cino had no doubt. However. . . .

3: DISCONNECTED BRAINS

... However, little by little, during his visits to the factory and during walks through the city, Sirio began noticing something that had eluded him at first.

And so every now and then the father would take his son along with him to the office, and sometimes his son's friend too. The driver would get in the front and they three in the back. This separation and all these details, which Sirio would take note of each time—though everyone pretended not to see them (as for example: his father could be as late as he wished, the driver always had to be on time; he and his father got in first, then Cino, the driver last; the driver would sit still for a moment, in silence, to let his father tell him which itinerary he had chosen; the father having spoken, the driver did not answer "Yes, sir" but simply executed the order, as though his father had spoken directly to the car of which the driver was merely a part, and not the most vital one)—all these details left Sirio with a distinct feeling: he was born different from the driver. He, Sirio, had free will; the other did not.

As they proceeded on toward the factory this discovery broadened to include everyone they encountered. Here is the traffic policeman who as soon as he recognizes the car halts all other traffic in order to give it right of way. Does that traffic policeman have a will of his own? There's the gatekeeper who from far away can be seen peering at his watch and looking right and left for some sign of the boss's car. Does that gatekeeper have a will?

The car arrives and the gate opens automatically. The car gone through, the gate closes. Does that gate have a will?

The father enters the hallway, the porter is on his feet at once, and the other employees, who have seen the porter stand up, stand up in turn without waiting to catch sight of the boss. That porter, those employees, do they have wills?

The boss and the two boys step into the elevator which is waiting there ready for them; an attendant, always on duty inside to open the door, shrinks into a corner so as not to take up any room. This elevator, that attendant— do they have wills?

Once while they were going up to his office Sirio's father had told him something funny and Sirio had started to laugh and, laughing, had looked at the elevator attendant's mouth, to see whether he too was laughing: no hint of anything, the man stood motionless, as if he hadn't heard. But he had heard. But his brain had not instructed his mouth to laugh. So the connections that went from that brain to that mouth had been cut. Who had cut them?

When the elevator reached their floor and Sirio and his

father stepped out into the corridor Sirio would immediately notice that in the corridor they were already alerted, all at their places, as if they'd known the boss was arriving—as if the building had transmitted the message through the walls. Those people, that building, did they have wills?

When his father sat down in his armchair, behind his desk with the telephones and the intercom keyboard in front of him, Sirio would ask himself: That intercom system, these telephones, do they have wills of their own? Yes, one did, and that was the red telephone, the first to the left on the desk, the one that had a secret number which was not listed in the directory and was not even known to the secretary, but only to the family, friends, and cabinet members. When that phone rang, the way his father picked up the receiver and brought it to his ear and the way he paid attention were altogether different from when he used the in-house telephones. First of all, it was the only phone that could ring there. The others rang in the secretary's office, the secretary got the name of the caller, what authority he had, and before connecting him to the boss would first ask the latter's permission by intercom: and so the only signal that reached the boss's ears was the buzzing of the intercom.

Were a directors meeting in progress—Sirio also sat in on meetings—no calls would go any farther than the secretary's office, and let there be buzzing or blinking on the intercom, the meeting would continue, as if that buzzing or blinking were inexistent. But if the secret phone rang, the one whose number was not in the telephone book, whoever happened to be speaking stopped at once and while the boss was answering—sometimes grave, sometimes jocular—everyone present at the meeting made as if he had disappeared, wasn't there, didn't see and didn't hear. Did those directors have free will? Had the wires from their brains to their ears been disconnected? Who had disconnected them?

But whoever was on the phone, who had called the secret number, who was making an interesting offer to Sirio's father (his father listened, serious) or telling him a joke (his father chuckled), he had free will, he had some power.

The brains of those who have power have all their wires intact, and some of those wires get connected to the brains of subordinates, employees, workers; who henceforth are not to act on their own.

Sirio had had the impression at times that when his father fired a manager it was because the wire connecting his father's brain to the manager's had broken and this manager, become disconnected, so to speak, from the body of the Company, was no longer able to be one with it.

And then it would befall the dismissed manager to spend a few months alone in his abandoned and cheerless family until he was hired by another firm, and when word of this reached Sirio's father he would think a moment about the boss of this other company, would think about the brain of the newly hired man, and would say "Yes, it's the proper place for him" or else "No, he won't last." He was never wrong. If the newly hired manager got along with his new company, then his family recovered its bearings and its vitality, but in a different light from before: the new boss's brain transmitted a different kind of charge.

While he was grasping these things Sirio also came to understand that in his turn he was going to play the same role his father played now: to have free will amidst a mass that did not, to sever the wires inside his subordinates' brains.

This was necessary in order to turn the pink lights on the map into red ones. On the map, the redder the lights of a street were, the stronger the Company's presence upon that street. The pink streets indicated sizable holdings; the orange streets better than fifty per cent of the property; red meant the whole zone had been taken over. On the map there were some twenty buttons he could push. He had to see to it that one day his son would have forty to push. If he succeeded his life would have a meaning. If he failed, it would not. He couldn't stop and call it a day without failing, just as a body cannot stop growing without beginning to die.

It was in the interest of all his subordinates: if the Company grew, all their lives grew and their families were more secure; if Company growth halted, all their lives wavered and their families trembled. Hence every day all the subordinates gave their energy, intelligence, will to the Company in order that the Company grow.

In return they would receive, once a month, their pay-envelope. The executives received it in their offices, on their desks, and it was an envelope with a check inside. The workers would pick it up at the cashier's window and for them it was an envelope that contained banknotes and small change in coins. The pay inside the envelope wasn't always the same, but being the translation into money of the subordinate's identification with the Company, it varied according to the degree of that identification.

If a manager had had a great idea, very useful to the Company, an idea that had led to a great contract, his pay would increase a great deal and might go on increasing regularly: and then it was called a promotion. If a worker had gone on strike, interrupting for a day or two his relationship with the Company and unhooking the wires that led from the Company to his brain, those days were not paid to him because the Company was able to transform into money only time spent living for it: the man went to the factory for eight hours every day, for those eight hours the factory took his life and transformed it into money.

Some managers and some workers were so pleased with this transformation that they would as soon have stayed on the premises permanently, would even have hidden so as not to be discovered by the guards who every evening made the rounds of each department and division to make sure it was vacated.

The end of work was signaled by a bell that sounded throughout the plant. As soon as the bell rang there were workers who would drop the work they had in hand and make a dash to get out. But there were also workers who would want to complete the part they were working on and would go on filing it, assembling it, drilling it. These would peacefully conclude what they were doing, carefully lay the finished part down, wash their hands, tidy up, leave last and in an orderly manner: every day they gave the Company a few extra minutes. The Company was aware of this and in the pay-envelope would give something extra in return, in the form of a bonus.

At the end of the month when everybody got his envelope everybody would instantly estimate what he had earned from the Company: the managers would then have a look at the amount of the check, the workers would feel the envelope with their fingertips and then stand aside to open it and count the money.

Sirio was greatly interested in this day—the 27th of each month—when the factory-employee relationship was weighed, evaluated and converted into numbers. It greatly interested him because he understood that the totals arrived at—the totaling was done in a very private office to which Sirio was one of the few who had access— would indicate how much wherewithal for life (for acquisitions, for expenditures) the factory was giving its employees for the month to come, but also how much life the factory had taken in the month just ended. There was something here that Sirio had not yet got altogether clear but was continuing to wrestle with. His father was of no help to him in this regard, for of this reciprocal relationship—life going to the factory, money going to the employees—he discerned only the latter term: money to the employees.

"This month," his father might say as they were driving home, "we have had so many billions and so many millions of lire in wages and salaries; a two per cent rise over last month. Therefore production has to increase."

His father saw only the money-out-money-in part of the give-and-take; the money-for-life transaction escaped him. To none of those who had founded and built up the Company in the past had the thought of this transaction ever occurred. Sirio had intuited it: then and there he knew that the factory, with him, was never going to be the same.

4: THE MIDDLE CLASS DREAM

When he realized Sirio had these thoughts his father drew him out upon the terrace and spoke to him as follows:

"My son, before you were born most of what you see did not exist. Men's lives were no happier than those of animals and no different from theirs. You know one world only and perhaps you find it banal. I knew another before this one and I find this world a miracle: the most splendid miracle wrought by man in all his history.

"This miracle changed man biologically: the children born today do not have the same impulses and the same behavior as their fathers: the automobile, today, has attained such perfection, such smooth-running grace that being inside one can only be happiness itself. Within fifty, within a hundred years, these cars will have an ascensional capability, they will glide about in the air in all directions, right and left of the skyscrapers.

"Once with nightfall life used to come to a stop, fear would arise. Now at night-time the city is awake, activity continues, children study, mothers work. It is as if life has doubled: my generation has given man as much as God gave to Adam. When the day began and it was time for men to leave for work, housewives would cross themselves: they'd pray that all this might never end.

"If you could look into the homes, the schools, the streets, you would discover that everybody smiles in the course of the day five hundred times more often than the previous generation did. Men of the previous generation were like animals, which never smile. They were born and then until they died they were sad. In those homes, in those streets, in those days and in those nights anxiousness was the only state they could ever be in: the mother became pregnant, and she was anxious; the child was born and the father and mother were anxious; the child grew, went to school, wanted to marry: and this meant anxiety for the parents because everything in life was dear, from birth to death one learned to do without two hundred times a day. Life had its price but nobody knew how to pay for it. Therefore everybody went through life not living and only those who were able to transform this constraint into acceptance could approach happiness. And all, when evening invaded their dark homes, lay in their beds, lined up and mute as corpses. So it was for untold ages; we have changed the world in the space of a few years.

"An astronaut from another planet, flying over Earth half a century ago and returning on one of these nights, would think he had lost his way: what used to be an opaque and lifeless globe now appears to him a luminous and indefatigably active globe.

"When one of us Westerners ventures into the heart of Africa the Africans take cover so as not to be found, they move off with the entire village: they foresee that upon contact with industrial man their lives and those of their wives and children would undergo an irreversible crisis, would be gripped by immediate convulsions, like an organism traversed by electrical current.

"A few years ago a French explorer discovered a new tribe living in a barely artisanal stage of civilization. He was welcomed with much warmth, was fed and cared for, and for a few weeks lived amidst a joyous people, surrounded by dancing from dawn to dark. He discovered forms of human behavior long since forgotten among ourselves and was particularly struck by the absence of competitiveness, of a sense of property, of pain: the males would offer him their women out of hospitality, and if a baby died, the mother would carry it off for burial with serene unconcern, without even informing its father. Surrounded by this blissful people the explorer asked himself every minute: Is this happiness? To answer this question he thought of coming back each year for a visit. When he returned the year after, the village was no longer there: vanished. Where he had been welcomed and entertained, looked after and served, there was no longer a soul. And yet no one apart from himself had set foot in the area. He realized then that his coming had had upon the tribe the effect a drug has when it reaches the brain: delirium. Once having set eyes on him they had all been unable to live without him. And setting off in search of him, the village had disintegrated.

"Yesterday I had a black man in here who was picked up years ago by a missionary and brought to this country to study. Now that he has finished his studies he came to me for a job: he doesn't want to go back to his people, and do you know why? Because he fears he will cause them unbearable pain.

"When a missionary arrives in some new village he discovers that two persons out of three have faulty eyesight: therefore, being unable to see well, they do not go hunting, they stick to well-trodden paths. But he does not give eyeglasses to everyone with defective vision, for not everyone is able to stand that miracle: some no sooner try on their glasses than they snatch them off, smash them into little pieces and bury every piece in the earth, because of their impression that the village, and not their vision, has been transformed and that if the missionary has the power to transform the village he might also make it disappear. Those savages have obviously grasped the truth.

"Once back in Italy, the explorers spend the rest of their lives puzzling over the behavior of primitives in the face of industrial age man. There are tribal chiefs who insist upon being the first to see the objects the explorer has brought and want to experience their effects on themselves in order to select which ones can be shown to the people and which cannot. On the printed book, the radio or the automobile it is thumbs down. They will accept food, a mirror, the matchbox. Only in three years, or thirteen, when they are accustomed to the matches, only then will they come near the book; and only much later the radio. They behave like a weary old heart confronted by joyous news: only by finding it out gradually, cautiously, can it survive, otherwise that news will be the death of it. We are the good news, the rest of the world is the weary old heart.

"Last week while I was driving down a street in an outlying district a man from those parts, an old man, nearly blind, threw himself under the wheels of my car, and do you know why? Because he wanted me to be responsible for his death so that I would feel a moral obligation toward his son and would take him on at the factory. As he was telling me this, gasping it out by the side of the road, I suddenly saw in him all the old men of his generation, by now irretrievably lost and destined only to disappear in order that, the world cleared of them, their children can grow up to be different. It was as though that old man was saying that his life meant less than his son getting a job at the factory.

"I am convinced that if a town crier were to go through the lands of the South, the peasant civilizations of the world, announcing that a young man from every family would receive employment provided an elder from each family were ready to die for this, I am convinced that half an hour later the son would be standing at the front door of every house, satchel in hand, with, at his feet, the laid out body of the elder displayed like a ticket. Industrial civilization is man at his spiritual zenith, the greatest uplifting man has ever known.

"There are men who, once they have entered the factory, are mindless of their own illnesses and infirmities; and they work, not so much for the salary which barely suffices, nor for the family which they rarely see, nor even for themselves: they work for work's sake and at the end of their lives while they have not accumulated anything for themselves, yet so purified are they by their years of work that they feel themselves different from others and only know and mix with their own sort, and they face death with this majestic pride and die in the hope that their sons will follow their example, and they ask that

their funeral be held in the evening, after the last shift at
the factory is out, so that those who attend won't ask for
time off from work. In their honor the factory whistle
blows twice.

"The factory today has the role that the church had in
the Middle Ages and I believe that just as during the
Middle Ages, and to this day in mountain villages, the
church has its little graveyard where they repose who in
this lifetime lived their highest moments in the bosom of
the church, and whose earthly existence would be mean-
ingless apart from the church; I believe that in the same
way it would be fitting today that the graveyard stand
nigh to the factory, because it is in the factory that men
find the meaning of their lives, and their hiring is their
confirmation, which makes them soldiers in the war of
production, a war whose battlefront is the same as the
battlefront of progress. Hence weddings and baptisms
should take place at work: the meaning of matrimony is
that it will produce new workers and baptism is the moment when a new man enters the world where one day he
shall work. There have been cases in the South where an
employee who was about to get married asked the manager's permission and introduced him to his future wife
because he did not wish his marriage or his wife to be in-
compatible with the factory. At the factory there will be
some ill-favored women, whom nobody desires, but if the
manager praises them, if he says they are among the best
elements working there, just watch if those women don't
have a dozen suitors within the hour.

"All this today applies to only a part of the world and
of mankind; but it is this part's moral duty to work toward its becoming the condition of the whole world and
of all mankind, and the fulfillment of this duty will give

meaning, not just to our lives alone or to our times, but to all bygone times: for all of history has been stamped by ill and in cancelling ill from the earth we amend all that has ever been."

5: THE BULL OF PHALARIS

As the father ended his speech sadness came over the son because not one word had convinced him. To what he had heard he answered thus:

"Dear father, among all the stories I learnt at school one in particular comes to my mind whenever I see a car, a refrigerator, a radio. It is the story of a tyrant by the name of Phalaris who ruled over the Sicilian city of Agrigentum. This tyrant was famous for his cruelty. Every morning he would make the rounds of his realm and point out a few of his subjects at random and have them put to death. And to anyone who might ask what harm they had done him his reply was: None at all; but have they done me any good? These words illustrated the conception he had of his power: the ruler must ensure that whoever exists, exists for his purposes. Whoever were to exist for purposes of his own must be considered an enemy and done away with.

29

"But power is not insensible. The tyrant's heart would feel pity when he heard the plaints of the condemned and the screams of the tortured. Therefore one day he called in his court engineer, whose name was Perillus, and said to him: I cannot stand the wailing of those I have put to torture; invent something that will render their cries tolerable to me; since the elimination of my enemies strengthens my power it should also be sweet for me rather than depressing. Perillus went to work and a month later returned with his invention and had it placed in the palace courtyard. What he had invented and constructed was a bull of bronze, of great proportions, big enough to accommodate inside it all the men the tyrant appointed to die each morning. Under the bull a fire was lit, in such sort that the bronze became red hot. Those inside would die in indescribable torments, screaming with all their might. But this was what the genius of the court had hit upon: in the throat of the bull he had placed musical strings, disposed so as to transform the exhalations of suffering into the sweetest sounds. This mechanism greatly aroused the curiosity of the tyrant, who wanted right away to see how it worked: having no one under sentence of death ready to hand he gave the order that the builder of the bull himself be enclosed in its belly and with his own hands he lit the fire underneath: and indeed from its mouth delightful music began to come forth, faint and intermittent at first, then louder and continuous but so pleasant and fair as to convince all who were listening that the person in there was not suffering at all, but undergoing the crowning pleasure of his life. Every morning thereafter the tyrant had a batch of victims collected and shut up inside the bronze bull and slowly burned: and the music of their shrieks, the sweetest music ever heard at court and in that city, brightened the tyrant's day, that of his guests and of his subjects. The moment of sacrifice thus became the happiest and most cheerful moment of the whole day. Hearing that music the palace servants and the court guests and the subjects out in the country-side would say: Our master certainly is not cruel, on the contrary, he is the most sensitive and generous man in the world who offers us such music, and we may consider ourselves fortunate to live under him. But with the pass-ing days and years the mechanism in Phalaris' bull wore down and the strings in its throat gradually gave out, and once in a while amidst the ecstatic music it seemed that a quaver of woe could be heard. Finally the strings broke and the music disappeared, the land was overspread by the cries of the tortured, the more unbearable because in Agrigentum they had all been accustomed for years to hearing nothing but perfect harmonies. So then the people understood the trap they had fallen into and they revolted, attacking the palace, capturing the tyrant and burning him alive in his own bronze bull. And so each and everyone, from its inventor to the sub-jects and to the master who had wanted it and used it, perished in that instrument: but only when the instru-ment had broken down could one say that inside it people perished; up until then nobody could suspect such a thing.

"Now, when I see the workers at work on the assembly line or the employees in their offices, all apparently happy to spend their lives this way, I have the impression that they are sealed inside this contraption which trans-forms their suffering and unhappiness into the music of industrial products that border on perfection. We hear nothing but that music: the cars by the million running in the city, refrigerators purring in every kitchen, television sets on in every living room. We have never thought that this music covered up the laments of entire generations. Here they all are, managers and designers, to prove with the sacrifice of their lives that this system produces happiness. But the system is already beginning to wear out and the first laments can be heard: the absenteeism from work, the acts of sabotage, the sickness fund. Whoever has come to realize that the system transforms laments into music cannot listen to that music one minute longer."

PART TWO: THE REVOLUTION

1: LEAVING HOME

So father and son had come to the realization that they were at odds. Everything the father had done, he had done for his son, but nothing of what he had done was acceptable to the son. All that the son was of a mind to do could lead only to the undoing of the paternal achievement.

"I believe that everything must change," Sirio would say. "I feel that if everything remains this way no one will ever be happy."

"You don't know what unhappiness is," his father would answer, "no one in your generation knows what it is: you have never experienced it. Before you were born everybody was in difficulty, there was no work, no food. Children were always sick. You wouldn't be able to live a single minute in a world like that."

"We'll never be able to understand the evils of that world because we did not live in it. But you are unable to

35

understand what is wrong today: troubles are coming and you are on your way out."

"You have everything we never had. We've devoted our whole life to this purpose: giving you all that we lacked."

"But doing so, Father, you filled up the gaps in your life and have made us into a reincarnation of you. We are not our own selves: we are your sons and belong to you. Everything that exists, you aim at possessing it; the meaning of your life is in possession. The life you gave us—in substance, you have taken it away from us."

Then the father realized that that son was not his son anymore and that he was no longer his father; he understood that soon his son would leave, nay, had already left, and that this discussion had taken place after an irreparable breach.

*   *   *

Having left the house Sirio began by calling upon his friend Cino. "I can no longer live under my father's roof," he told Cino. "I am the son of a factory owner, that is, of someone who's squeezed everything that can be got out of our society; and this situation weighs upon me like a sin I must expiate."

"I can no longer live in my father's house," answered Cino. "I am the son of an employee and this situation weighs upon me like a blot I must wipe away. When my father comes home and says: Today I worked two extra hours, I understand that he expects gratitude from me; but what I feel is humiliation."

"If I stayed I would become responsible for this sin and would perpetuate it," thought Sirio.

"If I stayed any longer I'd be providing further excuses for my father's work, that is, alibis for his exploitation," opined Cino.

And so both of them decided to leave home.

2: ON THE LOOSE

Once away from their families the first thing Sirio and Cino experienced was this: living away from home is not hard. A consumer society consumes too much and poorly: half its leftovers are still fit for use. And you are free. Sirio and Cino put a few days into getting accustomed to this freedom.

They had settled in a working class neighborhood where dwellings grew one on top of the other, so chaotically that the resulting architectural mess was something of which no map could possibly be drawn. And in fact these neighborhoods are unmapped. There lived workers, immigrants, pensioners, students. Sirio was overtaken by the giddiness a medieval man would have felt when, after having spent his whole life at court, he pays his first visit to the countryside: he sees such a variety of people, arts and trades that by comparison court life appears drab.

Their sensation of freedom came from the fact that

from the very first day Sirio and Cino discovered that living away from home was easy, and being easy was also agreeable. Very quickly they saw that food was everywhere: you had merely to take it.

Early in the morning, at six-thirty, before the coffee bars open, the bakers' boys go around town delivering bread, buns and pastries. They go about the streets leaving a trail of aromas behind them. Where a bar happens to be open they go in and leave the things on a table. Where the bar is closed they deposit the packets in front of the rolled down shutter. Passing by, you can lean over and take what you need: eat, eating's good for you. Throughout the apartment buildings errand boys are climbing the stairs, leaving the bottled milk, the packages of cookies, the folded newspapers in front of doors and on landings. They never make a mistake: at each floor they consult the list of orders they keep in a pocket. There, that does it: at the top floor they take the elevator down, whistling, or descend the stairs three steps at a time; out the front entrance they go, and down the street.

As of now in this or that six-story, eight-story apartment building there is breakfast for one hundred sixty, two hundred people. You can take your time climbing the stairs, choose what you like best, calmly come back down, eat.

If you run into someone, you go your way, he goes his: no danger at all. In the building they do not know each other; when one moves out and another moves in it is years before the rest of the tenants become aware of it; and nobody knows exactly how many members there are in the family above or in the one below.

So you can climb from floor to floor, look over the packets in front of the doors, read the labels on the containers of milk, verify the kinds of buns: you like that kind? it's yours, take it and go. You can look at the front pages of the newspapers, skim over the headlines; if something interests you you can take it along. Nobody will prevent you. Five minutes after you are gone the maid comes to the door to get the milk, there is no milk. She grumbles about the delivery boy having forgotten it, but it isn't a problem: the fridge is full of milk, for today there is even too much.

In school playgrounds, at streetcorners, in railroad station waiting rooms company men come by every morning to restock the machines that vend coffee, tea, orange pop, chocolate bars, cigarettes. The machines are patterned after a honeycomb: a wall divided into little cells. In each little cell there is something to buy. You press a button: inside the machine the wall moves and in front of the window appears the product you have selected; put a coin in the slot: the window opens, the product's yours. But you can make a hook out of a piece of wire and with it prevent the window from shutting: after that you can clean the thing out, cell after cell.

You don't hurt anybody: the damaging of the machine is anticipated and is already covered in the pricing of the products.

If you are looking for a bit of meat, a chicken, some cheese, go to the supermarket, pick up what you want and pay. Once you are out, take the most expensive product out of the bag, go back inside and help yourself to an identical package of that product: there's nothing they can say at the check-out counter, everything you've got is marked paid for on the slip, you are a model customer, a steady customer, eligible for a prize.

No dinner is complete without fruit. You can take it from the counters and eat it while walking: movement aids digestion. There are outdoor stalls under the arcades, at the corners of squares: you pass by, take an orange and put it in your pocket, two minutes later you can eat it at your ease.

If you need money it is everywhere. In the mailboxes, for example: before the mail is collected the boxes are full of letters, postcards and notes, just posted, all stamped: you reach your hand in and pull out a fistful, then you go somewhere else and remove the stamps. Every grab is worth seven thousand, ten thousand lire: a complete meal or two tickets to the movies.

Or else, if you prefer, you can lift coins from public telephones. You walk into a booth chewing gum, spit the gum into your hand and stick it up inside the coin return chute. Leave the booth and wait. Here comes a gentleman. He goes into the booth and inserts a pocketful of coins, he's making a long distance call. He makes it. When he's done he presses the button to get back the coins owed to him. The coins rattle in the machine's insides, you can hear them colliding, it's a sound of metallic rain; but instead of emerging they are snagged up in there: the passage is obstructed. The man hammers on the machine, punches the button twice, curses, and leaves. You may enter, the coins are yours.

This is a good time of day, if you hang around you can pull off the trick fifteen times in the course of an hour. You come out better than a working man.

You have the same procedure on trolleys, on busses: there aren't any more conductors, now they have machines instead: each machine takes in the money, gives out the ticket and returns change.

It's the same at gas stations, in laundromats. Here you pay with bills, you have to insert the bill face up: the machine sucks it in, reads it, retains it and gives you service.

But you can block the mechanism with a toothpick or a bit of adhesive tape: the bill remains pinned down or stuck on, moves neither forward nor backward. With a piece of bent wire you can then free it and pull it out: keep it, it's yours. You mustn't think that the last person who had it earned it in any better way.

Along with you in the same city thousands of people live by collecting what other people leave untended, bicycles, motorbikes. If the bicycle is fastened with a chain the wheel may be slipped off. If two motorbikes are locked together they may be loaded together into a van and, the rounds completed, quietly separated in a garage. No complaint will be lodged, and so no theft will have occurred.

Thus it is you can eat for free, you can drink, read, travel, you can have money for free. And you can have entertainment: every movie theater starts the last showing at ten-fifteen; at ten-twenty, having sold the last tickets, the cashier and the usher go home: you may go in and sit where you like, on the balcony or in the orchestra. No one will bother you.

Sirio and Cino quickly discovered that living for free, eating and enjoying themselves without paying is rather nicer than paying to eat and to enjoy oneself. Living and having fun in return for payment has about it something of constraint, something depressing, you are obliged to pay for something in order to have it, it isn't you that gets it but it that gets you. When instead to have something you need only take it, then it's really you who are in charge.

Away from home, their middle class families left behind, riches and careers forsworn, the two boys suddenly found themselves beholden to no one, sitting pretty on top of life.

3: WITHIN THE GROUP

Freedom is not part of man's lot. He is without freedom from the moment he is conceived: there is the someone else who thinks for him, guides his movements, every hour feels his developing body, photographs it with the sonogram, listens to it with a fetoscope. He comes into the world already having a nine months' history, a pre-history of nine million years. His whole future is channelled already: his professional activities and loves, sex and death. And that is where man situates his happiness: in not being able to think, in giving up thinking, in being what everyone expects of him. For years Sirio and Cino had gone on like that and believed that therein lay the meaning of life.

Now they found themselves in the exactly opposite situation. They could stay in or go out, go downtown or out of town, read or take a walk, be together or alone. Whatever their eyes fell upon they could take or leave. But above all when they came back they were free not to tell anyone what they had done because there was no one to ask questions. That was freedom: not having anyone to answer to.

When evening comes, after you have travelled for hours on the subway, after having crossed the city four times in all four directions, after having discovered what's new block by block—they have killed someone outside the stadium, in the center of town a sect is preaching the end of the world, as of today the private policemen in front of the banks are in pairs—when finally you get back home to a house that isn't yours and you think back to the things you've seen and the things you've done for which only you can approve or blame yourself, then you understand that you are truly free.

But someone living away from home, who has no address and pays no bills and whose whereabouts no one knows—that someone, actually, counts for very little. If he falls ill, no one aids him, if he dies they will discover his body by chance, as happens every morning in the case of vagrants and drug addicts.

Because they who relieve you of your freedom repay you for it every day in telephone-light-gas, in mailman-porter-cop, in airplane-elevator-streetcar.

Therefore whoever is outside society immediately forms another society, immediately seeks new companions to establish new relationships.

But your new companions also seek them with you.

If you want to find them you have only to get moving early in the morning, when the shift at the factory or the day at school starts. If you want to be found you have only to step outside the door, to be walking around your neighborhood in the evening after supper when plans are being made for tomorrow morning, or at dawn when they are being made for the day. Then you will run into those who bring the news, post manifestoes, hand out leaflets. You will receive information, appeals, instructions. You enter the circle.

So it was that Sirio and Cino had, more than once, come upon a girl called Carla distributing leaflets at a streetcorner in front of the nearest factory. Carla must have been an important person because she was sometimes handing out not just one sort of leaflet but two or even three. Stuff about a shut-down factory, an occupied school, a trial under way. One evening, coming home, Sirio finds her at the same corner, standing there watching people go by and once in a while singling someone out and saying something to him. When Sirio comes over she looks at him carefully as though deciding about him, decides yes and when he is near enough says to him in a murmur: "We are meeting tonight, join us" and gives him a mimeographed leaflet. Sirio walks away with the leaflet in hand and a thought in his head, and the thought was this: Why did she pick me?

That evening he goes, he wants to see what it's about. And, then, he is a free man and a free man is like an object where there is no gravity: a breath of air is enough to set it in motion. While heading to the meeting he feels that what has set him in motion was precisely those words breathed in his ear and not in everybody else's.

He arrives and someone is talking. Says that a worker will soon speak who was suspended recently. That cases like this one, in this one city, were more than three thousand in this one month and would double next month. He gets down from the table and disappears in the dark.

From the dark a worker arises and gets ready to speak. His head is uncovered as a worker's always is when he has something to ask. He says that his story is a short one; then he stops and rubs his nose. All expect him to talk about when he was hired, about his specialization, about his life at the factory, about the economic recession and about his being laid off. For centuries workers' stories were told in this way; and the remedy to their dramas was to be found in the labor union which was the negotiator between the worker and the factory. Instead, this worker says that he has a son now fifteen years old and his son is intelligent and studies, he's in high school, he wants to become a doctor. Here he stops and blows his nose. He says that he figured out how much money it costs for his son to study for a month and to get that money he is ready to do overtime, giving up his day off, and instead of letting him do overtime they lay him off, his son can't buy books and can't study. Because of this his life will turn out differently. Therefore when a worker has plans for his son these plans all depend upon the owner of the factory: if he makes a business mistake the workers' sons will pay for it with their lives. He blows his nose and steps down into the dark.

The worker's speech produced a deep silence in those present. There was something that had to be understood in that speech. That something was this: the system has not only your life in its hands but your children's lives and the lives of your children's children. Now, what had that worker's son done to the factory? Nothing. What had the factory done to him? It had altered his life.

Sirio was taken aback. What he had had so much trouble grasping—seen from the other side, was it not really crystal clear? For a whole period of his life he had thought that the best thing to do was perfect and perpetuate this system and it had been difficult and painful to realize that the system had flaws, and now he understood that everybody agreed that it was unjust. But if everybody had understood this, then it shouldn't be difficult to demolish the system.

Meanwhile another worker is up on the table, with his beret on his head. This one, probably, has nothing to ask for. He raises his right hand, rotates it so that it can be well seen by all, there's something about that hand, the index finger is missing. He lowers his hand and declares that he used to work on the assembly line, he'd take hold of the part that came along dangling in the air and would guide it to where it fitted into place. One day an improperly attached part turns up, when he touches it the part unhooks on one side and swings down like a blade. Under the knife was his finger. The factory changes him to another job, puts him on the control panel. At the panel he has to run the machines, throw switches, press buttons, pull on levers. But he's an invalid and whenever they need to suspend someone from work he's always the one. And so with the factory the more you give the less you have.

This worker says the exact contrary of what Sirio heard from his father. The factory is good, his father used to say, and gives to each accordingly to how much each has given to it. This man had given two joints of a finger and the factory's instinct seems to be to get rid of him. The first guy comes back to say some more. He announces that there will be a strike the next day, that it oughtn't to be merely a strike and that everybody should get busy so that it may become something more.

4: THE CREEPING REVOLUTION

From that moment on Sirio and Cino felt themselves a part of the Movement, in the thick of it. To have been in deeper would have been difficult and yet they wouldn't have been able to say how they had got there. The impression they had was that when you leave home to live a life without school and without work, all the friends you find are enemies of the world you lived in before.

When the meeting was over Sirio and Cino went to the Students House, in the university quarter, because that was where most of those who had been present were going. This way Sirio and Cino discovered what was, if not the revolution's heart, its nervous system.

They discovered that in the Students House they never sleep because there is always something to be done. The lights were on in almost every room. In some rooms typing was going on, you could hear the ticketytack of Olivettis as you walked by; in the hallways mimeograph machines were in operation, walking down hallways you heard the rollers whirring. In certain other places they were cutting and pasting, composing manifestoes, and exchanging insults while fighting over a concept, a phrase, a word. At three o'clock in the morning the Students House appeared to be a huge workshop going full blast.

And indeed that is what it was: for the activist committees, the proletarian patrols, the local cells, every kernel of revolution in the whole city had collected there: because there they could use the machines for nothing and find paper. They all have identity cards with photos that do not correspond to their faces: if in real life they are bearded, in the picture they are beardless, and vice versa. The clatter of the Olivettis keeps up until morning, then ceases to be heard, not because it has stopped but because it is absorbed into the daytime din. Going down the hallways, entering those rooms, picking up those manifestoes, those mimeographed leaflets, getting ink all over himself, Sirio had the definite feeling that anybody could get into the place, fascist or cop; could wander around, pick up information, read, without anybody noticing; could come upon any piece of paper, could walk off with it.

And so maybe some cop was observing, noting, spying. But what would it matter? The hundreds of persons talking, writing, printing would not have stopped on account of just one enemy; their faces could be so easily confused with so many other faces, they were unrecognizable; and the material being put together could shortly, at daybreak, be got hold of all over the city, without risk. Looking at those rooms teeming with activity, at the printed leaflets heaped in corners, at the people arriving in ever growing numbers (by now dawn was approaching) Sirio asked himself: Is this, then, the revolution? It was amazing: revolution was being born in the heart of the city, at state expense.

At sunrise all the chaotic movement centered upon the Students House promptly changed direction: the building that had been filling up hitherto was now emptying. The activists belonging to the various political groups who had come and worked all night there were now leaving with piles of printed paper and setting forth on mopeds and bicycles to hand it out.

Half an hour later the city suddenly wakes up and the busses start passing by every two minutes, letting out thousands of students in front of elementary schools, high schools, vocational schools, university departments and graduate schools, and now it is to the rested and quiescent spirits of those who during the night have only slept, who haven't listened to pirate radio stations and haven't watched dissident television programs, who haven't yet glanced at a newspaper, and if the world had been kidnapped during the night wouldn't yet be aware of it, it is to them that the activists—who all night have fought tooth and nail over a lead paragraph, who've telephoned everywhere for a scrap of information, who've been plying indelible marking pens, who've been running the mimeograph equipment for hours, who've helped each other and sworn at each other—those activists, worn out, nerves frayed, hoarse, now address this audience, crying their slogans, their appeals, their news. A languid crowd, taken by surprise, picks up on all this with a promptness that betrays thoughtlessness and absorbs it with a passivity that shows resignation. Thus does the creeping revolution advance, from day to day, from night to night, uninterruptedly, so there is no telling what point it has reached, whether it can still be stopped or not.

5: THE RADIO STATION

So far as Sirio understood this was the doubt that lingered in the activists' minds: they did not know at what point they stood. Whenever they organized a march, occupied a school, prepared a strike, they never knew what would happen, how long it would last, how it would end. Their wish was that the maximum would happen but the maximum was revolution and revolution is something one knows nothing about, for it is the reinvention of everything and hence, first of all, of itself. Unsure what it was and where it was but convinced that it had to be somewhere, those young revolutionaries—Sirio felt himself one of them—did what the enemy does when he tries to blow up a powder magazine whose whereabouts he has been unable to pinpoint: he fires everywhere. And so for years those groups and cells would take advantage of every opportunity history afforded: the economic slump, the suspensions, strikes, occupyings of factories; mass education, the uselessness of the diplomas earned, the

51

questioning of institutions, revolutionary curricula; the housing crisis, the evictions, the space lying vacant, those without a roof over their heads.

As Sirio could see, not only the leaders among the militants but all their followers as well lived in a permanent state of fever, awaiting the right occasion for massive mobilization, checking hourly on what was going on in the city, school by school, factory by factory, house by house. They lived interrogating one another on the telephone, monitoring local radio stations, taking notes, preparing maps. Sirio had no exact idea how one goes about making a revolution but observing those young people doing what they were doing he was becoming convinced that yes, one could perhaps be made that way. So let's have a shot at it.

The big strike due the following day could be one of those occasions that touches off a revolution; it could be the powder magazine. Therefore mobilization for that strike had been enormous, they had put everything they had into it. In the Students House the excitement was at such a pitch that there was no resisting the contagion: Sirio felt himself all atremble. And since everybody was printing flyers he started carrying bundles of them down the hallway to the entrance and loading them on motorbikes ready to take off.

As he was carrying one of these bundles, held together by a string, his eye caught a huge, screaming headline that read: "No to the tyrant owner!" That was his father. Leaving home, renouncing a career, going off to live on his own, he had done nothing other than say no to his father. What he was doing now was nothing but the logical continuation of that no, the putting of it into practice. That this happen was inevitable, it was right. The discovery that he was fighting not against an abstract system but precisely against his own father: not against industry and the factory but precisely against the Observatory interlude, against the luminous map ritual, against the Technical Bureau's secret projects, against the automatized movements of the Robot Squad, was disagreeable and painful, like treachery, but at the same time exhilarating, like a purification: and it constituted a sort of test of truth: you are never sure to want to make a revolution if you are unwilling to make it against your own people; and of that revolution the one you make against others is simply a forerunner. And of course when you make the revolution against someone, in reality you make it for him: to liberate him from what he is.

All night long Sirio carried leaflets, wrote manifestoes, put together slogans. The next morning with everyone already leaving the Students House, heading for the hot points of the city, he too set out and followed or was caught up within a small group on its way to the radio station.

It was a very small station, two little rooms and a larger one at the top of a pyramid of working class dwellings near the industrial zone. There was no elevator, you went up by a narrow and grubby staircase. After the last twist this little staircase was completely black, as if coated with tar.

It wasn't tar, however—looking closely at the walls, the ceiling, the steps, you saw that there'd been a fire there. And upon arriving on the premises of the radio station you discovered that the fire had been recent: two, maybe three weeks before. It must have been dreadful for not a corner had been spared, neither under foot nor over head. If there had been papers, wooden tables, plastic furniture, it had all vanished in the blaze. Probably started with a few cans of gasoline: the assailants would have come at night, you cannot close the gate down there at night because it is used by the families living in the same building, they would have come up the stairs in sneakers so as not to be heard, and carrying a few cans of high octane gas, reaching the top floor they would have got the liquid to run under the door, pouring it gradually, quietly, and then when it was all under there they'd have dropped a match on the very edge of the puddle: a flash and the fire would have been started. Then they'd have run back down and taken off.

When the first tenants wake up, roused by the crackling of the fire, choking on the greasy smoke, those who have set the fire are already in their hideout on the other side of town; there they hang on the telephone as the news is called in to them. They get the word on everything that is happening at the radio station; it's as if they were watching it on closed circuit television.

Here, the guys arrive, come up in groups, they swear, they shout. They shove one another, trade insults. They trade accusations. Someone rushes off. Someone else breaks through a door, any old door, the tenants inside start yelling, there are half-naked women, screaming kids, he doesn't give a damn, he simply needs to telephone, where's the phone? No phone? Another door stove in at random, same scene, but isn't anyone around here calling the fire department? Where's the phone? and quit screaming, here's the phone, bunch of assholes, it's for your sake also. Fire department? There's a fire here at the radio, you've got four minutes to get here, we'll be timing you on our watches, we'll be waiting for you in the street. Thirty seconds. We might have left someone to sleep inside, the way they do at Bologna. Sixty seconds, they sure aren't hurrying. If it had been a bank they'd be here already. Listen to it burn. It's all plastic. It'll be sixty million lire. We'll get it from our comrades in Milan. My ass. But we helped them when they had their radio burned down, didn't we? Worthless shits, they didn't even thank us. Ninety seconds. We should have left a group to stand guard out on the street, the way they do in Rome. You just don't know what the hell you're talking about. But they didn't get burned out, in Rome. No, instead they drove past on the street, sprayed the place with bullets and everybody out in front got it. A day of mourning. One hundred and eighty seconds. You still think they're going to show up? If they don't, those firemen, we'll damned well blow up their fire station. What's the fire station got to do with it? The thing to do is give the chief a lesson. He goes by every morning on the beltway, drives a red Fiat. What's important is that we don't get the police in here. Two hundred and forty seconds, four minutes, see what I mean? They aren't coming. So let's blow up the red Fiat and the fire station too, at this same time, exactly ten minutes past four, that'll teach them to be on their toes at night. There's a van going by, you want to bet it's those who set the fire coming back? Stop it, block the street, who's that inside? Ah, the first firemen, five and a half minutes, they'll pay for it.

What with assaults, bombs and flames the radio station is like Troy: destroyed and rebuilt many a time. A scholar who knew how to distinguish on the wall one fire from the other would read, concentrated there, the whole of the Movement's history.

6: Is This the Revolution?

There has not been enough time since the last fire to redo everything at the radio station: there are a couple of tables for the papers and documents, nothing to sit on, a heap of beers and cokes in a corner, some empty and some unopened. People are standing up or sitting on the floor. The broadcasting studio is over there. Small, soundproofed with plywood, it has a table with three microphones, a turntable with a pile of records, three stools for three speakers, a telephone. You can see it through the glass partition: there is space for six or seven people and there are twenty of them in there; if one comes out another goes straight in. Someone is speaking. He's yelling. The soundproofing isn't total because you can hear what he is saying. He's saying:

"Go in through Gate Four—I repeat, four, a few of our people are inside, they'll let you in. Four, " he repeats, "number four." Sirio makes this out to mean that the strikers are against marching on Number Four, that they're aiming at Number One, the nearest. But if they intend to occupy the factory they'll never get to the machines from Number One because to there you have two kilometers of internal roadways, buildings, offices, all garrisoned. "We know that," shouts a voice from outside: a series of lines, at least three, arrive at the radio station and they are amplified there and broadcast, "but they've got only a few dozen cops, we're four thousand marching in, once we show up they'll run away." Sirio puts it together in a flash: they obviously want to get in at the nearest gate, they don't know that today it is the most heavily protected; they want to get into the offices, forgetting that they are each one of them under tight security and that those offices aren't essential for the factory anyhow. Upon another occasion similar to this Sirio had heard his father exclaim: "Thank heaven they never go to the fuel storage tanks and the power plants." They've got to be told that, otherwise the whole thing's doomed.

The door opens, someone wants to get out, he has papers in his hand, he is unable to get through, he's being pushed away from the door, Sirio slips ahead of him before the door shuts, by the time it does he is inside.

The three receivers are coming in simultaneously but the speaker deals with them one by one, connects it with the microphone so that the voice coming in is suddenly on the air. "Situation, situation!" demands the speaker. The leader answers, his voice amplified, as though he were talking in the same room. Broadcast by the radio station, his voice reaches all the groups: those made up of workers who are marching on the factories in the industrial zone, crossing the pedestrian overpass, wheeling compactly to the right like an army on maneuvers; and those of students pouring into the university quarter, occupying the university buildings one by one, leaving patrols on the streets and at intersections. The voice of the leader guiding the column towards the factory is heard saying: "Can't possibly get through, all the police are here at Number One, jeeps everywhere. Guys, it'd be a massacre."

There is a moment of silence, during it everyone has the feeling the powder magazine won't blow up this time either. One can smell body odors become stronger, odors of sweat and breath. The speaker still has hold of the microphone but his hand is resting on the table, as if taking its time. It occurs to Sirio that the microphone there has the same function the luminous map has on the terrace of his house: press the button and you see the streets that are already yours, those that may become yours, and those belonging to competitors: you hold half the city in your hands, the other half you must conquer, this is the meaning of your life.

Slowly, as if there weren't thousands of people scattered about the city waiting for orders, information, directives, Sirio reaches out over the table, removes the microphone from between the speaker's fingers, raises it to his lips and calmly announces: "There is a secondary entrance, on the opposite side, giving onto the tracks. Over there, there are never any police." The three receivers on the table, which have been going nonstop up until now, suddenly fall silent and that silence gives the impression of a black-out. Then one starts functioning again and a voice is heard saying: "But the power stations are there." "Four of them," replies Sirio, "and a nuclear one. And that's the most vital point. Go in from the east side." Again silence and that blacked-out quality. News arrives from other parts: at the foundries there are scabs, they are operating at fifty per cent but that is offset by the paint shops where they have decided to stop work, it's being discussed, the management orders contingency measures put into effect, it wants to maintain a minimum of activity, this is where we are at now. At the Testing Facilities and Warehousing very few cars are arriving, practically none. It shouldn't be difficult to place a few thousand workers there, have them occupy the power stations from where you can paralyze everything. Here they are arriving: "We're at the sheet metal depots," "We're at Maintenance." Next to Sirio someone is marking the occupiers' advance on a map, Sirio sees the red line that has surrounded the factory bend to the right, then climb upwards, before long it will enter the area where the power stations are, there it is now: "We are at the telephone exchange," "We are at the first electric power station," "We are at the nuclear plant." At this point Sirio takes the microphone and quietly says: "Keep on straight ahead, to the storage tanks." The red line advances some more; through two generating stations on the right and two on the left, advances among a series of small circles: the tanks. Someone draws a big circle around the whole fuel storage area with a red marking pen: there the advancing line establishes a bridgehead. Telephones, electric power and fuel are in the hands of this mass of thousands of men who shortly, before closing ranks again, will cut circuits, shut down the electricity, isolate the plant. Without light, without fuel, cut off from the outside, the factory will come to a halt. And then we shall see. While contemplating this state of affairs and getting ready to think about what might ensue, Sirio is advised by the radio of three things: that a squad guided by Cino has been able to get into the offices of the management and that Cino, at that very moment, is standing squarely on the Observatory; that the forces of police that had been expecting the occupiers at Gate One, finally realizing they have been outflanked, arc heading in their jeeps for the power plants zone, that consequently being where the clash is likely to occur; and a moment before it was about to start, the first storage tank went up in flames, the others being certain to follow in very short order. Simultaneously the radio that was transmitting from the factory went dead and from then on the so eagerly awaited and by now raging battle was blanketed in silence, as if it were proceeding in another world.

7: THE YOUTH MOVEMENTS

Penetrating into the factory and ending up with a battle had been very easy and so could not have been very important. Perhaps it had even been counter-productive. According to the rare reports coming in it actually seemed that when the tanks had caught fire the workers had gone to work to put it out: the factory was their livelihood, to destroy the factory meant committing suicide for oneself and the whole family. That was not what they wanted. They wanted to renew their lives, not lose them.

Destroying what exists, starting with the factory, isn't to diminish poverty. The next day, for months and years afterward, all that factory's workers would have been poorer because it would have been necessary to put the factory back together at its former level of efficiency, and that would no longer have been high enough because other factories would have improved and progressed in the meantime.

That item of information—that the fire had no sooner broken out than the workers were struggling to extinguish it, the only definite and comprehensible bit of news that had managed to make its way through the silence of the radio—was for Sirio and all the others who happened to be in the broadcasting studio proof that everything had gone wrong, that the revolution was impossible, that before starting a revolution there was something else to be done: prepare the way for revolution, understand what it is, how much it costs.

That the battle had been lost was, in a sense, a piece of good fortune. Battles like that one were being waged just about everywhere in Europe, in Paris, in Germany: lost battles, all of them. So on the plane of relative strength these youth movements were still weak. Whence then did they derive their enthusiasm, their excitement, that energy that was causing them to burst out practically everywhere and, barely born, to multiply? These young people were animated by something that resembled fury: they were uncontainable. They couldn't be stopped. They could not be argued with: they were perfectly convinced they were right and therefore could waste no time in comparisons and discussions.

But precisely that was perhaps their contradiction: enthusiasm sufficed for them to explode in Italy, France, Germany, in Switzerland, in Rome, in Milan, in Turin, Paris, Marseilles, Bonn, Frankfurt, Zurich; but it wasn't enough to enable them to win.

The activity of the youth movements has led to a renewed questioning of everything: in the society of our day they have assumed a function that in a certain sense harks back to the movements in early Christian times and in the Middle Ages. Common to both the communist youth movements and the Christian movements was, as a central part of their doctrine and practice, the re-examination of fundamental concepts: What is salvation, what is sin? What is revolution, what is the bourgeoisie? What is one to do with oneself and with one's life? And in this re-examination it is implicit that the meanings proposed by institutions (Church, party) are false: stuff for pagans or for the bourgeoisie. The true meaning, awareness of which is the indispensable preliminary to one's liberation, is to be recaptured only by leaping back over years and centuries of accumulated theory and attaining directly to the source of truth.

Europe is alive with these bands of young people who, staging revolution, merely strike out upon the march that should bring them back to the great beginning, to the point from which communist ideology has deviated: a really meaningful start can only be made from there. Revolution is to young people's thinking as the Holy Land was to medieval Christianity: it is the goal and at the same time the point of departure.

The revolutionary youth movements being born all over Western Europe are like the crusades in medieval times: they represent the purification of an epoch. But just as the crusades were an impossible purification and moreover finally constituted the moment of maximum contradiction between Christian practice and Christian principles, and therefore a mortal sin on a massive scale—crimes, slaughters, tortures, conquests, money-making—so the young people's revolutions of today represent the crisis of communist revolution in the world, its impossibility, its uselessness.

Along with the crusaders went merchants, rogues, adventurers, professional soldiers, fugitives from the law, children escaped from home, offenders of every description: and the purifying crusade became the orgy of sin and not one crusader could be absolved by any confessional in the world. Into our revolutionary groups enter the sons of the upper class, the rich, the well to do, common delinquents, bored students, kids run away from home, drug addicts, scientific researchers, university professors, who when the revolution fails will rejoin the ranks of exploiters, heads of this or that, managers, administrators, that is, the ranks of the middle class: and at bottom they've never left off being middle class and the revolution is the magical thrill needed to conjure the monotony of their solid middle class situations, guaranteed by their firm hold upon society. Were a true revolution possible, the lot of them, taken one by one and brought to justice, would never be spared by any tribunal of the people.

Great is the harm that they wreak. Because, all the while proposing the return to the source of truth, they do not create a stronger union but set in motion a process of breakdown and successive divisions in so far as it nullifies what has been believed up until now and has functioned as the coagulative nucleus and absolute guarantee of unity: its source. The need for unity, so compelling in all revolutions at the moment in which they become institutions, itself turns up as a barrier, triggering the self-defensive mechanism of excommunication, of proscription, of persecution and of repression. The Neo-Christian movements that flourished during the great revivals of Christianity, isolated, excommunicated, dispersed and persecuted as they were, could not have resulted in anything but their own annihilation. There was an error in their constitution and in their practice and the violent end they came to was on that account inevitable and, in a certain way, merited. The revolutionary youth movements, intervening to create splits and produce a crisis within a workers' movement that has lasted for three quarters of a century and now has its liturgy and its rituals, deliberately provoke a reaction and in the ensuing collision the only thing that can result for them is their own undoing. The Church could not absorb the heretical movements: for the Church that would have been like incorporating a blasphemy into the body of the liturgy and transforming its ritual into sacrilege. She had no choice therefore but to extirpate heresy by force of arms, with a general mobilization that did away the hesitant and the neutral as well, in order that the phenomenon be forever prevented from recurring. Pacified after the great domestic crusades, the inquisitions and the massacres, the Church could look upon the slaughter just accomplished as the price that had to be paid in order to rise innocent and sinless once again: a blood baptism that purified her in the eyes of the Almighty.

The collision was not an accident met with in the course of things but the conclusion at which every heretical movement aimed. Similarly, the repression the youth movements encounter in the world does not stem from the intolerance and the errors of governments, for were governments to change tactics the youth revolutions would intensify their provocations: because it is direct confrontation, violent conflict they seek. To obtain it they have kidnapped industrialists, assaulted police headquarters, sequestrated ministers, set fire to schools and factories, blown up automobiles, trains and barracks—whatever was required. Had it not sufficed, they could have gone further, aimed at kindergartens, retirement homes, individual dwellings: there is no ceiling to the level of provocation, all you need to do is persevere. The effect of all this was to shift the confrontation from the plane of political and social rights to that of force: in the matter of rights the Neo-Marxist movements were not completely mistaken and some of their charges against capitalist societies and real and official communisms can today be seen as straightforward historical truth, as were, yesterday, a good part of the charges the Neo-Christians hurled at the official religion and its ruling hierarchies, including the accusation that the Pope was guilty of simony.

However, the Neo-Christians' achievement, though positive in the religious sense, was negative with respect to religion because it did not strengthen religion but served only to precipitate a crisis within religion. Likewise, what the young have achieved through their revolutionary movements, while positive in the sense of their critique of Marxism, is negative in the political sense because it disunites the working class sector, creates rifts within it, weakens and paralyzes it. And it enables the other side to come away victorious without even having to fight.

*   *   *

And that's just what was happening, right then, in the battle going on in the big factory in front of Cino's eyes: reacting to the fire at the storage tanks and the power stations, several hundred workers had turned into firemen and were toiling to keep the fire from spreading to the adjoining areas.

The police, come in great numbers from all over the

city and drawn up in defense of the administrative offices, stood by and watched. The battle was over. Therewith began the hunt for those responsible.

*   *   *

The map in front of Sirio in the broadcasting studio and which until then had permitted us to follow our friends' advance into the enemy's heart—the nuclear power installation, the electric power stations—now served to follow their retreat. The occupation of the power plants and the setting fire to the fuel tanks were to have been the catapult that hurled several thousand enraged workers into the cerebral zones of the factory: that was to have sent the factory into a coma. But this did not come about. It was not the workers' wish that the factory burn down and perish. They did not want to lose it. They wanted a world without bosses, not one without factories: as soon as they saw the factory in flames they saw themselves ruined and actually betrayed. To urge them to go farther, to storm the administration buildings, would have been exceedingly dangerous now that they were regretting having gone as far as they had. That is why the rank and file's incentive to push forward was suddenly gone and at the very same moment the guidance ceased from those few who were inciting them. That precise moment, which was to have marked the high point of victory, marked the beginning of defeat. While one side realized it had lost, the other side instantly understood it had won: the police started advancing.

The workers who were there felt no misgivings when their identity was checked, for they considered themselves completely innocent: they hadn't set the fire. They didn't know they were in a trap with no way out: they, and only they, were where a crime had been committed. So their fate, for the time being, was to be put in jail; what would come next remained to be seen.

Cino was arrested upon the Observatory itself: from there he had witnessed the whole thing, the mass of workers invading the courtyards, then the succession of fires breaking out one after another, by induction: he had stood there transfixed by amazement and disbelief. When they led him away, one policeman on his right, another on his left, he went on staring at the flames (red-black) as if spellbound, inwardly repeating a question which had already become an answer: But could it really have been so easy?

Sirio at that same moment was emerging from the radio station where the other speakers went on describing the fire at the factory as the working class's greatest victory. On the way home he went on asking himself: And now what?

PART THREE: FIRST LOVE

1: FALLING IN LOVE

Three months later, by chance, Sirio met Carla at a conference. Specific charges continued to lack against almost all those still in jail, the police being unable to document the specific crimes of each prisoner, and in the city this had left behind a train of suspicions which gave rise to debates, appeals, protests. Every other day a conference was held. And at one of them Sirio met Carla.

The hall was full—there were many parents and relatives of the prisoners—Sirio was toward the back among those standing up. A lawyer was speaking. Every now and then some spectators got bored and left. At one point Sirio saw someone stand up and turn around to leave and it was Carla. And as soon as he recognized her he realized that it was somehow an awaited sight: without being aware of it he had been waiting to see her, and among the multitude of those he remembered seeing since he had left home, in the students quarter and since he had been

71

taking part in meetings and struggles, if there was one face that kept reappearing it was Carla's. He knew little about her, had barely heard her speak, and yet he had wanted to see her again, had even dreamt of her. And roaming about the city from morning till evening without ever encountering her he had come to suspect that she had moved to some other town or had landed in jail. But no, there she was, she's right there, she's free. That face with its broad cheekbones, those steady and as if recently awakened eyes, that thick mane of black hair, that indolent and listless way of moving, that face of a squaw, everything confirmed that it was she, that she was there; and watching her go past Sirio repeated to himself over and over again: "It is she, she's there" and felt a contented feeling because he felt he would see her again.

*　　　　*　　　　*

He saw her three days later, at an art exhibit. The exhibit was set up in one of the university courtyards and the paintings were hung against the walls all around the perimeter. They were disarmingly ingenuous paintings, but it was to be a charity exhibit and therefore all had to be sold. Charities (theatricals, lotteries, exhibits) rest on this basic understanding with the middle class, that what it spends, it spends for itself. If it's to aid the insane, it's to keep them far away. If it's to aid missionaries, it's so they can extend the frontiers of its religion and of its civilization, in short, of its life. If the middle class buys a picture at a charity exhibit, it aids a painter who's not its enemy. Terrorism was petering out, dissolving into processions, demonstrations, strikes; the middle class was getting its courage back, organizing theatricals and exhibits everywhere: that exhibit was in one of the university court-yards, and there was Carla. She was sitting on the little wall from which the columns rise and two monks were coming toward her, walking slowly and conversing in low voices, each with a coin in his hand. There in a corner was a Coca-Cola machine. While inserting the coin and wait-ing for the bottle to come out, it seemed to Sirio that they each cast a fleeting glance at Carla, looking at her for a tiny fraction of a second, like a camera, but that's what made him suspicious because he foresaw that later, in their cells, they'd take their time fiddling with the photo in their hands. He watched them go away, heads stooped, sipping their Coca-Cola through a straw. I am jealous, he thought, therefore I am in love.

He went over towards her. When he was in front of her she raised her head. She was like before except that she had a sad, bitter expression in her eyes and on her face, something that, without diminishing her beauty, gave her a suffering air. She's not been well, he thought, no telling whether she's over it. He sat down beside her. "Hi," he said. "Hi," she answered. They looked at one another in silence. "You want to go out?" she asked. They got up and went out into the street.

Down the street a student demonstration was coming. Those in it were moving unhurriedly, pushing mopeds and bicycles, laughing and shouting, waving red flags. Someone among the demonstrators called out Carla's name. "I have to go," said Carla, excusing herself, and she disappeared into the crowd.

Left alone, Sirio continued on in the opposite direction to the demonstration. "I don't know her address, but I'll find her again," he thought. And out of curiosity he looked at each of the front doors of the houses he went by. And as he was looking he discovered something he had never noticed before though he'd come that way many times: it was a street where Jews lived and next to the resident's name (Ederle, Levi, Bergamo, Civita . . .) was written, unfailingly, in black, in capital letters, the word *Jew*. In the case of buildings made up of apartments, where there was more than one name, the qualification *Jew* was written beside the uppermost one only and then was recalled underneath, next to each name, by ditto marks. The column of family names aligned one below the other seemed like a roll ready for the call.

*   *   *

Lost in thought, he noticed only belatedly that he had arrived at his house. Since Cino's arrest he had been living alone and the house served only as a place to sleep. He'd remain at the Student House until midnight, then go home and read an assortment of newspapers, and finally stretch out upon the bed, still dressed, listening to the radio. But at two o'clock in the morning he was more wide awake than ever and decided to go out. Not that he was thinking about Carla, but he had just seen Carla again and he would start to think about everything and be unable to stop what he was thinking. Better to go out.

The whole city lay asleep; one could meet with the unexpected at every turn. That the city was totally asleep was revealed by the fact that even the tramp was sleeping. The tramp was a foreigner who for the past few days had installed himself under the arcades with an entire bed. He must have been around fifty to ninety years old, with hair so long it got tangled up in his beard, purple skin from a cirrhosis of the liver. He was under the arcades, lying under blankets and on top of a mattress that was on top of another mattress, which was on the ground. His was the immobility of the recent or imminent apoplectic attack.

The arcaded street where the tramp lay continues for five hundred yards and comes to an intersection. At the intersection there is a bank whose entranceway is flanked by a series of shops.

The shop windows were dark but enough light came from the streetlights and the traffic lights to read the prices of the clothes and of the record players and what the lire was worth in foreign currencies. All those rates are yesterday's, thought Sirio, at opening time they'll update them. He felt himself enveloped by a shadow and turned around. A man in a green uniform with a big pistol on his hip was looking him up and down from one yard away. He moved on, turned the corner and went up to have a look at the shop window there. In it was a big placard, a lady putting pots of geraniums out on a windowsill: "She loves the house because it is hers" said the words underneath. It was home loan advertising. He thought about that lady's husband and said to himself: He loves his house because the woman is his. He felt enveloped by a shadow and turned around. A man in a green uniform with a big pistol on his hip was looking him up and down from a distance of one yard. It was the same one as earlier, but he realized it was the same one not by his figure or his clothing but from his expression. A little before when he had turned around to be greeted by that stare, the thing he hadn't been able to move on away from and get free of was the order that stare communicated.

He'd known at once that there was no way to talk, to say hello and to ask anything. That stare was saying: On your way! But it wasn't only the stare saying it, everything was saying it, the pressed uniform, the creased pants, the perfect tie, the red beret.

Everything was saying: I don't sleep, no one gets the jump on me. And now with that obtuse, square, opaque, determined face there in front of him for the second time he felt the order was being repeated, irritably: something like: I told you, on you way! If the words had been actually uttered it would have been less effective. Instead he had merely come up, noiselessly (he wore shoes made out of canvas, tennis shoes) as though to display himself as there, uniformed, and armed. In that ensemble the gun had enormous importance. It explained everything.

The man wore a red tie, his beret was red. Together. That meant he ran no risk of losing his cool, got into no fist-fights, the beret never fell off and no one pulled off his tie. He fired, and remained in appearance as faultless as before. He was above physical force. He represented another kind of force. And that force was saying: I'm telling you, on your way. But he himself was silent and this was worse because it meant: I don't need to tell you; on your way.

Sirio understood that he had no choice and set out toward the center of town. Reaching the second intersection he turned left, but had taken only a step or two down the new street—very straight, narrow and empty, like a furrow run between the buildings—when two men, until then crouched down on the ground (wayside posts, that's what he'd taken them for) sprang up and drew shoulder to shoulder to block his path. The street was poorly lighted, a few small lamps swaying high over head, glowing inside a shroud of phosphorescent mist. No getting through this way. This way lay MSI headquarters.* He

* Movimento Sociale Italiano: the Italian neofascist party. (Tr. note.)

faced about and while looking for another street to take he told himself that those two armed men were not the same thing as the bank policeman. To begin with, there were two of them. And instead of: On your way, these were saying: Don't take a chance by coming closer. They were not reoccupying an invaded camp; they were holding it against invasion. They didn't come up silently behind you but took up position in front of you. They were defending something that, from the point of view of those who are armed and commit violence and keep others at bay, meant more. The bank was worth one guard. The MSI was worth two. The bank was worth a reconquest, the MSI was worth a preventive defense, waged to the death. In the bank window you can look at the lire exchange rate or at the terms upon which they'll give you a loan to buy a house. But you cannot get near the MSI windows, see who is going in, coming out, who works there. They won't even let you onto the street. By night the city has all her streets except one, for this one ceases to be hers.

I want to be alone tonight, I want to be able to think about Carla, Sirio was repeating to himself as he proceeded toward the central square. There he saw a man emerge from a building with a dog on a leash, the dog was wagging its tail because of the cold, it approached a pillar and lifted a leg. Then it was trotting along shaking its head, with the man holding the leash remaining plunged in sleep. They soon disappeared around a corner. They reappeared by and by, went in through the entranceway they had come out of and vanished up the stairs. Along that same street a group of youths was now arriving, a small group, four or five—not five but four—who as soon as they reached the square stopped and looked about, calm and self-assured, standing shoulder to shoulder.

There was nothing and nobody apart from Sirio and all four therefore focussed their eyes upon him. There was nothing strange about this but there was something strange in those eyes, as if their gaze was not content simply to see. One, at the back of the group, was chewing, that designated him as an underling. The second one was a bit shorter, he was the calmest of all, and that one was the leader. The one in front was in front by chance or by mistake. Indeed, he slowly withdrew, shielded himself at the leader's side, then took another step backward and ended up behind him. There was someone on the square, the leader had to see and decide.

The leader was looking and that look was saying: I must decide whether to let you be here or destroy you. Sirio felt as though a sentence was about to be pronounced upon him and that sentence corresponded to the offence of being, by night, on that square. At night one is in bed and asleep. At night the city has its masters, like those standing in front of him, and they could let him be or destroy him. He was not guilty of anything, he was not competing with them for possession of the city or a share of it, he did not want either to write on walls or set fire to buildings or shoot or mimeograph leaflets, he only wanted to walk around and look, but perhaps they had understood this well enough and perhaps it was just this they did not want: they were the masters of that part of town, they did not want to be seen in action by somebody else. He was guilty of having seen them.

To make up for what he had done he slowly retreated, walking under the arcades, in the shadows, and he headed for the basilica.

Yesterday he would have accepted the challenge but today he had Carla on his mind, he did not want to think about anything else.

Before he thought it was within view he caught a glimpse of the basilica. Lofty, imposing, illuminated by yellow spotlights. It was out of place, like an archaic word in modern speech. Thus isolated by the light of the projectors, thus detached from the rest of the city, it seemed to be floating. Sirio gazed ahead.

He heard, gradually approaching him from behind, the strident sounds of a motor and he stepped aside to let it pass. But the car drifted up and came to a stop alongside him. In it were two uniformed policemen, one at the wheel, the other in the seat next to him. They stared at him attentively, the way a doctor peers at a symptom or a magistrate examines a file. That stare was saying: We've been driving around all night, and here you are, we see you.

Embarrassed, he took a step back and retired under the arcades, so that they would leave. Is it prohibited to look at a basilica? Aren't tourists allowed to be out at night? Can't one pause during a stroll at five o'clock in the morning, and stop in the middle of the street to observe? To have moved over onto the sidewalk was tantamount to saying, humbly: All right, I'm moving on in the direction I was going, you can do the same. But they weren't moving on. It seemed as if they were fishing in their memory for a face resembling his, assigning him the past, the record of someone who was wanted, the search for whom was now at an end. With their memory they were leafing through their identification album, but turning the pages slowly. They were turning them backwards now, maybe there was someone in there that looked like him. He wanted to prove his innocence, to say: By night we all look alike, but if he spoke it would be worse, they would get out of the car, and as he understood this he understood, instantly, what he had absolutely to avoid in this encounter: he had to avoid their getting out and questioning him.

By now in the course of that nighttime walk through the sleeping city he had understood a good many things: that he was in love, that love rendered him different from other people, because the others did not have to cope with bank policemen, MSI guards, night warriors, whereas he did; and that this difference rendered him sleepless, made him go out for a walk, visit squares and churches, and this rendered him suspect to the police. When the police find someone suspicious they immediately look for him in some identikit: the way a doctor, presented with an illness, tries to recognize it from the books he has read. But if the police find themselves looking at some unknown fellow, without a past, who's doing something strange, they have the satisfaction of the doctor who, peering through his microscope, exclaims: What do you know! a new virus!

That's right, he was a new virus. Nowadays the city was full of old viruses that covered the walls with red and black inscriptions and readied mimeographed leaflets for dawn. He was different: in the middle of the night, peaceful and awake, he looked at the basilica (thinking about Carla, but this the police could not know). He behaved by night as if nighttime were daytime. If a tourist looks at the basilica by day a policeman passes by and says to him: Pretty, ain't it? But if one goes around in the middle of the night and pauses for some quiet contemplating the police come up and wonder: What crime does this one have up his sleeve? Because the night is designated for sleeping, if one sleeps by night then one can work by day, but if at night someone stays up and wanders around and contemplates, either he is a burglar or a terrorist or an absentee and if tomorrow he goes to work it'll be to commit an act of sabotage.

He withdrew still further into the shadow and proceeded slowly toward home. He kept listening to hear if the car had started up to follow him. His feeling was that it had not and he imagined the policemen had remained inside consulting with one another. Probably they had pulled out the identification album and were going through it looking for his picture. One was holding the album and was flipping the pages, the other was shining a light on the photos and sketches. The police Alfa Romeos have a special lamp, connected to the battery, for reading maps and documents: he knew this because he'd spied on the patrols at work.

Since falling in love he had already learned a whale of a lot. He needed to get back in a hurry so that he could think it all over in peace. If just then someone had asked him what being in love meant his answer would have been: discovering the world.

Now that he was heading home the city was beginning to wake up, in each building the lights were on in windows and where the windows were of different sizes, the one that lighted up first was always the smallest, and in the apartment houses where the lighted windows were more than one he noticed that they were always in a vertical row, and he understood that they were bathroom windows. Employees and workers would get up and eliminate the night. Then they turned off the light and five seconds later turned on another: the kitchen. Once the night had been eliminated they ingested the day, starting with coffee. There ought to be a special radio in every household, switched on by the employers, to direct life in such a way there would be no waste or nonsense.

Get up, the employers say, go to the toilet, you have four minutes. Flush, switch off the light, go to the kitchen, have breakfast, you have six minutes; kindly snap into it, it's late. Get dressed. Better not to wake up the wife and children, that can cost you time. Get a move on now if you please, out into the street. Leaving you can slam the door so that the wife wakes up and gets the children ready for school. Run, there's the bus. The wife wakes up and finds herself alone, understands that the day has started. What then was there before? Before was the night, the grandiose, fabulous, suspicious night. It brought police patrols forth, under its protection guerillas marched, leaflets were printed, dogs and nightmares wandered abroad. The night wrote on walls, it kept watch over banks and political parties. But of this no one must be aware, there must be just enough time for the sleep and rest needed to recuperate the strength of the previous morning; he who is able to do this can consider himself well off. The city was waking up, neurotic, psychotic, it moved in jerks and starts, like a train after a stop, and he was slipping along through the streets (Via del'Ospedale Centrale, Via delle Cliniche Universitarie), minuscule and mysterious, like a virus in the X-ray of a lung.

2: BEING IN LOVE

The next day he woke up with an immense longing to see her again. He still did not know where she lived, he didn't know her last name either, nevertheless he had to see her again, right away. He dressed in a hurry and went out. He was walking fast but he did not yet know whither he was heading with such confidence.

Two or three streets later, by then in the vicinity of the university, it suddenly came to him: he was going straight to the place where he had met her the day before. If she too is thinking about me she'll have come back, he was thinking. He entered the university building, crossed the first courtyard and stood in the second one, where the exhibit had been.

It was empty. Actually there was only one person, sitting on the little wall, in a corner at the far end. It was Carla.

He sat down beside her, looking at her. She had a

guilty smile, as if she had been found out. He was looking at her from eight inches away, then four, then he lightly touched her with his mouth. She was trembling a little. He went on kissing her, rapid fire, all over her face. Now professors and students were walking by all around them, it must have been an interval between classes; they came and went, talking busily, seemingly oblivious to that love scene between two young people.

They remained thus locked in embrace, almost as if they were hiding in each other, for an hour. Then they stood up, perhaps to find another place. A few steps brought them to the university movie theater which was open on mornings.

They were showing *1900*. She stopped to look at the posters and it seemed to him that she wanted to go in, not perhaps to see the film but to be in the dark. They who are in love are in another world and the dark nullifies this one. In they went. They took two adjoining seats at the back. They were holding on to each other as if to keep from getting lost, without saying anything. When Sutherland killed the cat by attaching it to a plank and smashing it with his head (a furious encounter, he loses more blood than the cat does) she turned suddenly away from the screen, Sirio wrapped her in his arms and hugged her and thus both forgot about the film which ended in due course and the lights were turned on. While the audience rose to leave they two remained in each other's arms for yet a little; finally she raised her head and looked about, much bewildered at finding herself in a movie theater. She did not remember her fright of a while before. Love had protected her.

(That day upon returning home he wrote opposite the date on the calendar tacked behind the door: Day of the Smashed Cat.)

*　　*　　*

Hence on that day the Smashed Cat is commemorated. The next day is that upon which the Rin-tin-tin is remembered. He realized that he had entered the territory of falling-in-love as if into a maze: he could become lost because none of his former experience mattered or helped in there; this was a different world entrance into which meant undergoing a radical transformation.

What is the Rin-tin-tin? Here is the story. That day they had an appointment at eleven in the morning in front of a bar, L'Ippopotamo. He got there at seven-thirty and went in. He sat down at a table. He had them bring him breakfast, three or four newspapers, then he pulled out a notebook and made some notes. The idea had occurred to him to keep a diary. From seven-thirty on he looked at his watch every five minutes. But she was taken up, and arrived as she had promised at eleven sharp. He saw her in the street, through the glass, and for a moment sat still and watched her. He liked being able to watch her unseen.

She was walking to and fro on that brief stretch of pavement in front of the bar, nervously glancing at her watch. Every once in a while she would stop and turn to look the other way. When she turned to look her dress would pull taut, revealing the shape of her body underneath. But it wasn't this that merited attention. The necklace she was wearing around her neck merited attention. It was a chain. Not a little chain but really a chain, heavy and big, yellowish against her purple sweater. With each step she took the chain swung forward, always falling back to the same position, that is, into the cleft between one breast and the other, with a little clinking *tin-tin*, like that. He was looking at her through the glass and for an instant he identified himself with her, and felt the chain strike its little blows against his breast at each step: *tin-tin,* like that. At one point she turned her body quickly round to the left and stopped. Owing to that movement the chain swung in the right-left direction: gave a little tap upon the right breast, a little tap upon the left breast, then fell back in between. *Rin-tin-tin,* like that. The time was 11:02.

That day was to remain forever Rin-tin-tin Day: to be inscribed upon the calendar, replacing the saint's name there.

*   *   *

Two days later as they were walking arm in arm down Via della Torre Vecchia and he was telling her some story, not especially funny or anything, just some story or other, with just one comical point in it, Carla burst out into loud laughter. Such a burst and so loud that he stopped, startled. It was an extraordinary event, he hadn't foreseen it. When a fellow goes to see his girl friend, even when they are just starting to go out together, he knows inside what can happen that day and what cannot. That is why he is her boyfriend and she is his girl friend. He had never thought she could laugh so openly because until that day she had maintained a course of sorrowfulness. But he was happy that she had laughed so loud and within himself he decided at once that he would call that day Day of the Ha-Ha. Actually not only the day but the street also: Ha-Ha Street. Rue du Ha ha—even better in French, actually.

*   *   *

When something memorable had taken place, something that deserved to be noted on the calendar, he would have a feeling of fright: his fear was that on the same day something else just as memorable might happen. In that event, he decided, he would note it on the calendar, yes, but shift it to the day before or after, so that each day was characterized by one event only, filling it entirely. Two events within a single day would both become minor events, like two saints on the same day.

*   *   *

Knowing Carla was, for Sirio, to become worldly-wise, and filling up the calendar with events meant filling up his own existence. All this seemed to him to be nice, pleasant, to have a meaning which, actually, he took to be the meaning of his life. And he felt that his life up until then—when he was moving toward a career, when he was thinking about revolution—had a meaning precisely because it had led to this, to knowing Carla and becoming her boyfriend while she became his girl friend. Love left no room for anything else. He considered it luck to exist during the years she existed. He might have been born a century earlier or a century later: what misfortune! But he was born around the time Carla was born and destiny had brought them together: from this event his life emerged so deeply transformed that henceforth nothing could ever be as it had been before. Carla was everything and this everything was his alone and was never enough. And as by degrees he came into possession of it (walking at her side, going to classes or to the movies with her, riding on the same bus, taking her back home, where Carla always had to return because her mother was unwell) he felt himself being transformed as though he were introducing a chemical agent into his system. Carla, taken in daily draughts (in the form of look, words, gestures) was setting in motion an unstoppable psychic reaction; and all this was called love and for a very large share of human beings of all races (white and black, red and yellow) it is the highest experience and most radical transformation—that is, revolution—in the whole of life. Often the only one, because sufficient.

*   *   *

Right away he had begun to suffer from an obsessive and groundless jealousy that drove him to want to keep everything for himself and almost to lock her away bodily. Just hearing someone talk with her inflexion upset him, because it almost seemed to him that anyone who borrowed her way of talking could steal her speech, could enjoy her words, and, since talking is a manner of making love, if she were talking amongst people who understood her words it was as if she were making group-love. There were moments in which words attained an intimacy so secret that no act of love could have brought such a communion into being. Moments like these could occur anywhere: on a streetcorner, in a classroom, in a coffee bar. The attention with which she greeted his words, as if they were long awaited, showed a disposition to love beyond anything a body can suggest. Looking around him and observing the passers-by he had noticed that long-established couples speak languidly, that is, they love each other languidly, out of habit: it's as if in bed the knee of one bumped some private part of the other without either of them noticing it. Young people, on the other hand, speak to one another with a vivacity that becomes aggressiveness, vehemence, frenzy: they manipulate words like weapons, they wound each other continually, they do not yet know how their bodies are constituted, their mode of dealing with one another is continual attack and continual reconciliation. To him it seemed that speaking to her was another form of loving her.

His was a fidelity that applied not only in the present and the future but looked toward the past as well: it would occur to him that he had never before uttered those particular words, never before employed that particular tone, never before asked those particular questions. In a certain sense he had kept them in reserve. Words never before pronounced would come to his lips, but this was possible only because he had never pronounced them before. He had known that Marisa now had a lover. Marisa was someone who worked at the radio. To him it seemed right: so tall, with defined cheekbones, with a small round mouth, with her hair done in a very long braid and forever astir with little movements this way and that as if it were alive with a life of its own—it was right that Marisa be much loved, that someone devote a year, two years, a few years to her. But Marisa's entire existence would live upon the interest of those few years. He knew Marisa's lover: slightly myopic, slightly bald, always wearing a tie, he taught at the university now and acted as if he owned the city. He found it right, normal, that Giulia had a lover. Giulia ran a little bookstore in the student quarter. With red hair, with high, large, firm breasts, with her scurrying about as if she were always late and that rather silly smile of someone who has been caught in the act. He knew Giulia's lover: somewhat short, dark—dark hair, eyes, complexion, clothes—a heavy-lidded gaze, wrinkles under his eyes. He worked in a bank. The sensual type, capable of loving for a couple of months without thinking of anything else, but who then climbs into bed with a cigarette in his mouth and in his hands a pile of accounts to be gone over, to be momentarily put down on the bedside table should lovemaking seem unavoidable. Yes, these people loved: normally, wholesomely. But he was doing something different: he not merely loved, he loved Carla. Therein lay the difference. He felt he was acquiring an added significance not because he loved but because he loved Carla. His existence lay not in love itself but in the cause and object of his love: Carla.

There was something attractive but tormenting in the idea that Carla was unique, that no one would ever see the likes of her again. This thought made him love her more but with a sense of loss or perdition, of defeat, of helplessness. How much happier is the normal love of ordinary people: those men who work in banks or teach in universities, who to their own surprise love a woman for a few months or a few years, inadvertently get her pregnant and have their minds elsewhere, on friends, male and female, on work. Another woman more or less similar to her mother would be born from that absent-mindedness, between then and age twenty would attract the attention (for a few months, for a few years) of a bank clerk or a professor, who would love her, wondering at his own feelings, would impregnate her inadvertently, would then transfer his thoughts elsewhere, to friends —male, female—to work. This alternation of attentions and distractions forms life and history, creates families and nations, and constitutes what is called normality.

*   *   *

Sometimes it befell that he saw or ran into Carla by chance. The influence of these chance occurrences upon his life was enormous: they persuaded him of her omnipresence: as if Carla might be everywhere. To have met her where he didn't expect it led him to expect her everywhere. He started to scrutinize the knots of people in front of shops, boutiques, supermarkets, libraries, outside movie theaters, to examine the crowds at public assemblies, at demonstrations, at marches. Every time he'd see a group of people come together upon whatever pretext (collection of signatures against an MSI meeting, protest against the arrest of some comrades, occupation of a school, sale of clothes imported from India) he would go up as if interested in what was happening but in reality because he was guided by a question: What if she were here? In this way he began to think of her in all places and on all occasions, but sometimes concluded that yes, she might be here, and sometimes no, she wouldn't have stopped by here, if by mistake she has she'll have left right away. He could not tell precisely what must have made her leave but felt there was something about it here that didn't fit with Carla: the words, the clothes, the way of eating (groups of people squatting down are always eating something), the way they addressed one another. From one thought to the next he came to realize that he was getting to understand many new aspects of Carla, and finally to understand her. It could be that Carla spontaneously tailed after a group that spoke and behaved in a certain way, it could be that the group itself behaved in one way without Carla and differently with Carla. Thus, wending his way through clusters of students in front of cafeterias, strolling alongside processions, he might think: Carla can't be here or Carla isn't here yet or Carla isn't here anymore. These were not only means to keep his own desire of her at bay; they were means to understand her. Understanding a person is an interminable operation, it lasts more than a lifetime.

*   *   *

Carla was now going to class again like a great many other young people belonging to the Movement, so numerous that the university could no longer contain them within its old buildings and therefore had to construct new ones. The new institutes were going up, notably, in the residential areas, the greenest, the airiest ones. There was, moreover, no other place where one could still build. So clinics, gymnasiums, schools and, naturally, little villas were sprouting up out there. And there arose the city's biggest old people's home, surrounded by individual dwellings for the newly rich and supermarkets selling food and electrical appliances. At the edge of that neighborhood stood a police station with the Gazellas* out front, always ready to rush to the scene of the latest purse-snatching.

It is a big home, separated from the street by a tree-shaded front yard, so that the elderly, if they wish to be out of doors, are exhibited to the passers-by, the local residents who built the home for them. And the old people sit flung back on the benches, drinking up the last of the sunshine, mouths agape and throats quivering, like lizards on the little wall, and the lawyer driving past in the Alfa rolls down the window and looks them over and

* Police cars. (Tr. note.)

Being in love

feels generous as he thinks to himself: The sun, they get that courtesy of me.

Carla went often to that neighborhood now. And Sirio accompanied her or went there to pick her up. That neighborhood saddened them both, a great deal at the beginning, subsequently less and less. Sirio came to understand why: Carla's presence in that place wrought a kind of improvement there.

When he had understood this he sought a way to make the improvement complete, and he found it. One day he had a rendezvous with Carla at the end of the street. When he saw her off in the distance he slipped out of sight and let her walk up and down for some time. Meanwhile he calmly observed the surrounding area: each house with its antennas, each yard with its dog.

Carla, uncertain and uncomfortable, walked farther and farther away until she was beyond the church. Finally he moved out into the middle of the street and waved to her. She answered by lifting her right hand and, perhaps, smiling, and immediately started toward him. He waited for her without stirring, letting her proceed step by step past the Fresh Air Compound, Soup Kitchen Alley, the Church for the Aged and Derelicts Boulevard. Only then did he advance to meet her, and outside the Infirmary they embraced at length. She was wearing a red jacket, sleeveless and buttonless, over a short-sleeved white blouse. While they were clasping one another he turned his head and looked for the last time at the street, the church, the home: street, church, home of Carla Wearing Red. The whole neighborhood had been regenerated forever.

*　　*　　*

Upon her head Carla never wore anything and in his usual picture of her she was bare-headed. But here she is one day in a yellow kerchief, a big bright yellow kerchief that covered her cheeks and hair and was knotted under her chin. What had happened? And since she was carrying a furled umbrella, sepia but with abstract designs printed in various colors, he looked about him and understood: it was late autumn, the sky hung so low that the antennas on rooftops seemed to be piercing it. The season had suddenly changed.

In the city it is hard to keep track of the seasons. There is no grass, there are no trees, there are no birds. The city is the psychiatric hospital of nature. One cannot discern nature in the city save in the form of caricature. One cannot know what season and what month it is other than by looking at the date on newspapers at home or on the clock at the office or on the towers of the public square. The seasons can be divined from advertisements: store windows display bikinis, newspapers illustrate holidays, we are in summer; the TV shows overcoats and raincoats, hence it's winter. But to offset this imperfection of nature there was Carla: Carla indicated the change of seasons by means of sleeves, blouses, buttons, jackets, boots. This was therefore autumn rain Carla: yellow kerchief and sepia umbrella. But there would be the winterish Carla (maybe a knitted coat: grey, grey-blue), springlike (maybe a wrap-around skirt held with a safety-pin) and again summery (a light-colored blouse, collarless, like a moujik).

He felt that to love meant to know: love is a form of knowledge. In this knowledge of everybody and everything knowledge of one's self was included.

He felt there were obscure symbolic relationships be-

tween knowledge of Carla and knowledge of himself and
of the city, relationships not everyone could understand.
He saw people happy when he was happy. He was happy
when Carla was. This kind of happiness was just content-
edness to exist. It was as if a round of questions and answers was going on inside him: Am I happy to be in the
world? Yes, because there is Carla. And is the world
happy to be in the world? Yes, because it contains Carla.

*   *   *

One day at the beginning of winter a smiling Carla
came running, with a bearskin hat on her head. One
couldn't understand why she was smiling, but thinking it
over, the why of that smile was in the picture itself: the
bearskin hat. Carla was smiling because she had found a
bearskin hat. She was smiling because she could see herself. In showing off there is always an element of self-
observation. But in this case something more subtle was
happening: in the showing off was included self-observa-
tion through the other's eyes. And in fact someone on the
street had no sooner seen Carla wearing the bearskin hat
than he had smiled. And she too had smiled, as if she had
seen herself with the eyes of that stranger.

*   *   *

During the hours when he was alone in that tiny apartment in the students quarter he would think about what
had befallen him, he would try to make out the design of
his life. Every once in a while, once a month, when he
obtained permission, he would visit Cino in jail. They no
longer had much to say to each other, but Sirio had un-

derstood why: Cino had changed too. More than a year
had passed since his arrest, but as yet no precise charge
had been preferred against him; and this without anyone,
any radio, any newspaper taking the matter up. And so
Cino too had made the bitter discovery that he was alone
and had realized that in two, in twelve years, he would be
unable to talk to anyone about what he had done, because
he would not be understood. Cino was cut off from the
world and in the meantime the world was changing.
Keeping him in jail served precisely that purpose. At their
last meeting Cino hadn't even opened his mouth: he had
come to the visitors room, had sat down and started
looking off to the side as if absorbed in private thoughts.

*   *   *

Sirio's thinking was fixed upon Carla. He thought
about her all the time; to put it better, whatever he might
be thinking about, at bottom he was thinking about Carla.
Carla had invaded the whole of his life. Once in a while
she'd drop by his place. The first time she came it was an
afternoon, he was waiting for her at the door. He wrapped
his arms around her there in the doorway and then, without loosening his hold, guided her, with wee little steps,
into the kitchen, and taking one of her hands had her
touch the door, the gas stove, the dishrack, the sink (there
was water in it and she got wet), the window, a chair, the
table, another chair, the door; he guided her out again,
holding her so tight she was hardly able to move her feet;
he had her touch her hand to the door, then to the book-
case, sliding her hand over the spines of the books, then
over the table, the chair, the lamp, over more books, one
of them lay open and he moved her index finger over a

word; he brought her hand to the light switch, turned the light on and off, guided her to the corner where the studio bed was, had her touch the pillow, the sheets, the head of the bed, then picked her up with one arm under her shoulders and the other under her knees, laid her down upon the bed, knelt down next to her, kissed her in the center of her forehead, then upon the right eye (her eyeball moved), then upon the left (that eyeball moved), then on the neck (she was breathing), then on the right breast (called Tin), then on the left (called Rin) (making Rin-tin-tin), (at that selfsame moment he was thinking: So this is where the meaning of life is?) then he drew her up to a sitting position, then lifted her to her feet, then took her out hugging her tight, guided her hand to the doorknob, to the hallway wall, the door to the bathroom, the water heater, the toilet seat, the edge of the bidet, the shower faucet (it was dripping, she got wet), the mirror, the soap (it landed on the floor and slid across the floor as if it were a wind-up toy), the comb (it was broken), the sink (it was dirty), the doorknob, the hallway wall, the entrance wall, guided her hand to the door handle and pressed it down. She remained for a while like that but felt the door opening and when it was open felt him let go; feeling herself freed she took a step backward, continued to move backward until she was detached from him and through the door, which slowly shut.

Passing a place where he and Carla had once met he had thought: *È bello*. Beautiful. The word, thought and not spoken, had the effect upon him of an electric shock: because *bello* did not at all apply to the place (a short and narrow street, closed at the far end, with overhanging balconies not far above his head) but to Carla. It was as if he had said *Carla è bello*. In that *bello* there was something embarrassing, but it was an embarrassment that was exciting, not painful. His excitement indicated that he was on the brink of a new discovery and the absence of pain foretold a discovery that was not painful. He let himself go, slowly, and closed in upon the discovery, gradually. First of all he felt that *bello* is larger than *bella*, more ample. *Bello* contains *bella*. This struck him when he tried to amend his thought and say: *Carla è bella*. Though grammatically correct, this sentence said little. All it indicated was Carla, from head to toe. But he didn't want to say only this, he wished to say more. He wished to say that Carla's beauty extended to the environment, to the narrow dead-end street, the low balconies. Carla with everything surrounding her was *bello*. That everything, which has its center in Carla, is *bello*. It is no longer in the feminine because it is no longer Carla alone, but has become *bello* because Carla has become everything. This was a difficult and complex thought (the Carla that is not feminine but neuter) and he decided he would never communicate it to anyone, not even to her.

*   *   *

At dawn he heard the confused sounds of the city emerging from sleep like a whale from the sea, that din created by the hundred thousand noises of other existences that provide the background to the noise of your existence. The idea came to him at once that amongst those hundred thousand existences there was also Carla's and that maybe she was already up and about and getting dressed. He said to himself: Carla is up, and he too got up, with an alacrity that pointed to a desire, the desire to put his life in synchrony with another's, as if to make them one. If he succeeded in doing this, that is, if he had the impression he had achieved this oneness, he would feel a kind of serenity that bordered upon euphoria; if not, he would feel disturbed and as if diminished, as by the discovery of an imperfection in oneself. It seemed to him impossible that another woman had ever been loved more than Carla was. It would be like asking that the day last more than twenty-four hours. No, to love more than this was not humanly possible. Actually, this was already no longer love: to love was being added something that resembled mysticism, that sought or accepted the submission of the self.

Adults who love for the fourth or the fourteenth time love in a practical manner, elegantly, with a sense of humor. Young people, in their first go at love, love mystically.

*　　*　　*

Nowadays in the Movement's press he also and especially read the letters sent in by readers. His first question was: What is Carla to them? He'd pay particular attention to how it was signed. Each young person's story was summarized in his signature. There were signatures such as "A blown-away from Bergamo" and he would say to himself: He doesn't have Carla; or else "A spy" and he'd say: He's lost Carla; or "Che Guevara" and he'd say: His Carla is far away; or "The nun from Monza" and he'd say to himself: She's Carlaless. This last thought sent a crazy proposition running through his mind: two people who love one another should register at the town hall with the same name, for example Carla and Carlo. They would like to introduce themselves to friends saying: "Carla,"

"Carlo," which means: "He's my boyfriend," "She's my girl friend," "He's my man," "She's my woman." And how can they do this? They go to the town hall and they say: "She is Carla. I want to be Carlo." The mayor stands up and says: "In the name of the people you will be called Carlo," and so he is her man and she is his woman in the eyes of the world. At one stroke the world would lose half the names of the people in it, two and a half billion. For mankind it would become two times easier to know one another. This is called revolution.

*   *   *

In the newspapers there are letters written by fathers saying "My son has run away, I didn't expect it." He interpreted it thus: fathers do not love their children, if they loved them they would write: "I knew my son wanted to run away and I secretly helped him." The father helps his son to flee but the father remains behind as a hostage to pay for the flight. The son who returns is the son who has been caught: his plan for running away was not perfect. Must do a better job of it the next time. Revolution always starts with a running away. So did his: he ran away from home, and from that moment his life began. He'd also known that from that moment things at his father's factory had begun to go badly, and he felt that the students-children's revolt had a lot to do with the fathers-industrialists' crisis.

3: How Love Dies

And so Sirio had fallen in love and this love had absorbed all his attention and had estranged him from the world. During all that time he had not known what was happening around him. When were his comrades going to be put on trial? How many had been fired at his father's factory? How many exams had he still to take?

Slowly, with the passing of time, these problems regained importance; Sirio became interested in the news once again, began attending meetings and simultaneously felt that this being in love was subsiding, was turning into simple love, which no longer sufficed unto itself.

*   *   *

Where he lived, in the part of town dominated by the university, the night was never peaceful, there were always groups moving hither and yon, jeeps on patrol, watchmen making their rounds. There was no sound of traffic: this was heard by day. For the most part they were sounds that had to do with writing: typewriters typing, duplicating machines duplicating, and there was that continuous rumble of young people tramping from this apartment to that, from building to building, from street to street. It was as if at night the city stopped producing and doing business and concentrated upon writing and communicating. The night was the exact opposite of the day: by day the city was all work and no words, in offices and factories the word was tacitly banned, by night the city was nothing but words whispered or written or printed. When Sirio slept, he slept amidst this hum. When he went out he felt his thoughts become entangled in the network of other people's thoughts, like radio waves interfered with by too many stations transmitting at once. But it was like this for everyone else.

If the students were organizing an occupation to begin at daybreak and if instead of thirty of them being up there were three hundred, the entire neighborhood slept less soundly and for a shorter period. If the police, instead of passing by every now and then in a jeep and confining themselves to taking infrared photos of the picket lines in front of the institutes, set up roadblocks at intersections, conducted a search at the Students House, captured a few fugitives and took them away under arrest, not only the students in the house but the entire city got no further sleep: word of the bust quickly reached the militants of the Social Centers and the Agitation Committees, who convened in their respective offices, mobilized the rank and file and prepared the retaliation. Police patrols were suddenly extended throughout the neighborhood, the watchmen outside banks and party headquarters, the private guards outside newspaper offices and the homes of manufacturers were suddenly on the alert and edgy. A scrap was coming, a siren went off, the police radio stations were broadcasting nonstop, throughout the whole city the level of sleep suddenly fell and the city was in a state, so to speak, of unconscious alarm. So it was whenever, for example, students set a car on fire, burned the rector's study, took a laboratory in the Department of Chemistry by assault. Or whenever a patrol of Blacks* had approached and come to grips with a squad of Reds. The Blacks own the squares in the center of town, the Reds own the outlying squares and the university zones. To go in daytime from a red zone to a black means going through an invisible political customs; anyone can inspect you, from inside the bars, the shops, from behind windows, from parked cars. You have to change uniform, get rid of your eskimo** and walk differently, pay attention. You are reminded to do so by the posters, the inscriptions on the wall, the faces around you. At night it's better to cross those zones one person at a time, never in a group, and in a hurry: to go through is permitted, to dawdle is suspect, to stop is dangerous. It's wiser to keep in the middle of the street, to keep away from the arcades. Let yourself be seen, don't avoid streetlights. If a car turns on its headlights don't lower your eyes, don't shield them with your hand. Those are the rules, you cannot change them, either obey them or keep away from there. But it had always been like this. For several months he had forgotten about it, now he remembered. During those months he had lived in that city and in that time as if he belonged to another city and to another time.

Now he was making contact again.

* Right wingers, fascists. (Tr. note.)
** Army surplus anorak worn by left wingers. (Tr. note.)

*   *   *

One day, a Friday, he was to go to the university with her but it was the last Friday of the month, the day when he could go and see Cino in jail. He went therefore to see Cino, who was worse than usual, and forgot about Carla. The next day he saw her by chance, on a street in the center of town.

Seeing her again after that missed rendezvous and observing her from afar he wondered how on earth it had been so easy to forgo a meeting with her.

Rather than surprise he felt that there must be a reason, a weak point in the power of that figure proceeding along at a distance from him, on the other side of the street. But the weak point was perhaps only in the fact that the relationship had been too close. There hadn't been a moment's pause. By error, by chance, by fate, by necessity, somehow this fusion had been interrupted for a moment and in that moment doubt had slipped in. While he watched her vanish in the crowd he felt that that woman was beginning to interest him less and would end by not interesting him at all, because with her everything had happened, from the casual encounter to appointments, from discussions to love. What he could now receive was ever less, perhaps nothing more. He had improved streets, squares, classrooms, he had rebaptized streets. He had rediscovered the city's past, had understood the people who live in it and who had lived in it. He had stayed up at night, prowled around like a stray cat, had got himself noticed by the night watchmen, by the groups to left and right. He had had some sort of fever and during this fever had had visions and heard voices. Perhaps he would never forget what he had seen and heard, but probably he would never see and hear it again.

The meaning of life had shifted elsewhere.

Part Four: Self-Awareness

1: ARTIFICIAL PARADISE

When everyone had ceased to give it a thought the date for Cino's trial arrived. Since his capture along with twenty other comrades, the day of the fire at the factory, much time had elapsed. During this time Cino had received three separate visits from the examining magistrate but had failed to grasp what he was actually being charged with. The first time the magistrate came in he read to him from a stiff sheet of paper where there was mention of "an armed band" and at those words Cino's reaction was more of surprise than protest. "Armed?" he had exclaimed. The magistrate interrupted the reading, folded up the sheet of paper, placed it in a folder, and left. Cino did not see him again for a year. Cino began to wonder whether some of those arrested that day had indeed been carrying weapons, and he tried to guess which ones.

For a few months Cino was put into a cell with avowed terrorists, five of them, who had actually shot and killed and who, they too, were awaiting trial. Much puzzled, Cino was forced to take note that for them he was a terrorist of the same stripe as they; none doubted in the least that the revolting things imputed to him were true.

They adopted this principle: each one of us has done everything he has been accused of plus a lot more of which we shall never speak a word so as not to aid the Government. And so in the cell there was never any allusion to terrorist undertakings, killings, attacks, fires and robberies, other than by nods, winks, innuendo and scornful laughter. Cino had the impression that if they'd been accused of some inexistent outrage, for example, blowing up Mont Blanc with all the skiiers on it, they wouldn't have lifted a finger to defend themselves.

There were five of them but they formed a very united group. This was to be seen upon every occasion. For example, upon the arrival of the newspapers. When the papers arrived, early in the morning, they would scour through them with a nervous avidity, searching for any articles of interest and would pass these to the leader right away. They weren't five: they were four plus a leader.

During the exercise hour in the big courtyard, swampy and forlorn, the others moved about, jogged or did exercizes by themselves, whereas they always walked clustered together, the leader in the center, as if to protect him from who knows what.

This behavior was something new in the prison and this novelty drew the attention and a sort of respect from the other prisoners and even from the wardens. The wardens' respect was illustrated by this: whenever they had something to deliver to the leader they would address him as "Professor."

During the time he shared a cell with them, Cino realized that he was the object, at least to some extent, of the same attention and the same respect; they treated him better than the others. This pleased him. Deriving pleasure from it, he took good care not to show that he had nothing to do with them. And so he was considered, and considered himself, one of the group. And that was a group of avowed terrorists who had never known any language other than armed violence.

When, a year after his first visit, the examining magistrate called upon Cino to read him the entire accusation, the phrase "an armed band" got no reaction from him: it was a perfectly normal accusation, it would have been strange and even dangerous and for that matter humiliating had it been different. Specific facts, in the accusation, were not mentioned.

And so something befell Cino that is frequent in the world of justice, of crime, of trials: a man who has committed a crime but who is at large, amidst people, feels that he is innocent; a man who has done nothing but is locked up in jail begins to appear and to feel insecure, to hide the truth, to modify his relations with everybody else, to behave like a culprit.

This transformation is facilitated by the fact that the State that jailed you under an accusation would like to see that accusation confirmed: to reject or fight it will cost you an effort every day, to resign yourself to it will not cost you anything further. And like many of the others awaiting trial, Cino had resigned himself.

Furthermore, in jail you have to choose at the very start: either you fight or you resign yourself. Those who fight are for the most part the political ones: they draft proclamations, compile reports, scrutinize the press, write to journalists, receive correspondence: and at the end of every day they have completed a mountain of research, of studying and of drafts for programs to put any manufacturer, university professor or statesman to shame. At day's end theirs is this satisfaction: to have outproduced the other side. And their companions' satisfaction closely resembles that of those who assist in scientific research: they have put their brains in tune with their chief's, they've enabled him to work better and produce more: it's been a good day.

Those who resign themselves have a different problem: passing the time. When you spend an indefinite amount of time waiting for justice, the problem of how to pass the time becomes a different problem: how to eliminate time. But this is not a problem that is born in jail when you arrive there: it is born when jail is born. Therefore it is a problem that jail has always known about and to which, over the ages, it has already provided many solutions. You have but to accept the most recent solution jail has found: drugs.

The five terrorists who were in the cell with Cino were transferred to Rome, to appear at a trial where they were cited. Truly, there was not a single political trial with which they were not connected, and they very well knew why: during the years they were fugitives from justice they were systematically incriminated in every criminal attempt that was committed, this to oblige them to come forward with denials, to defend themselves, to expose themselves. They'd never fallen in with this scheme and so, when they were caught, they ended up being accused of practically everything and were shunted from one trial to another, from one city to another, from one prison to another.

Prison inmates speak a language of their own, make up a world that does not communicate with the rest of the world. The man who has to spend his entire life in prison begins to think about prison exclusively, to know a city solely by the type of prison it has, to adopt for prisons the names they have in prisoners' slang. Thus San Vittore is "The Lombardy Shithouse," Poggioreale is "The Slaughterhouse" and "The Graveyard" designates Asinara because "whoever ends up there shoots himself." The best prison is Rebibbia, known as "La Dolce Vita" because it is full of prostitutes who at night sing songs, are rowdy, converse with their men who call up to them from the street outside.

Not without astonishment Cino discovered that his five terrorist cell-mates knew the menus in all of Italy's prisons and had greeted the news of their transfer to Rebibbia with outpourings of joy, because that is the place where one eats best. At Rebibbia their stay was to be relatively brief, just while the trial lasted, but Cino would not see them again and so for him they would always remain in "La Dolce Vita," and after their departure, around evening, he sometimes imagined all five seated side by side on a bench, the leader in the center surrounded by the others, newspapers in their hands after the fine supper they had just had, listening to the prostitutes chattering away in Roman dialect with their men down in the street. And so the months of close contact with these terrorists, five exponents of the guerilla warfare which had infected Italy for fifteen years, were completely useless to Cino and finally banal; from them he learned nothing, got not one idea, not one analysis, not one project; he had only understood that prison, even prison for life, would not break them down; they had a boundless capacity for

adaptation and resistance and because of this would survive physically: from now until five, until fifteen years
from now they would continue to live, work, study in
prison with the same obsessive sterile passion. Maybe
every five, every seven years they would publish something: an analysis of their defeat, a new call to battle, a
critique of official communism, an appeal for the re-
sumption of arms.

But if yesterday one such message had a thousand
hearers and today one hundred, tomorrow it would have
not even one: completely incomprehensible. For a lifetime they'd continue sending out senseless communica-
tions, and this is known as madness. Their moving from
one prison to another, from one trial to another, issuing
proclamations, was in reality a wandering through the
underground meanders of madness until winding up lost
in darkness and silence. Of their work in the world there
remained, as enduring scars, dozens of dead bodies and
thousands of imprisoned ones; nothing else. They had
appeared in the cities of Italy with the same effect as a
mortal epidemic. To have known them, to have shared
the same cell with them for months and months, to have
read the same newspapers and commented upon the
same articles, to have shared the same exercise hour with
them, walking in the courtyard in the same group, and
especially to have been charged with the same misdeeds
and to be awaiting a similar trial, all this for Cino meant
feeling like one of them but also meant measuring the
distance separating him from them, and enabled him to
feel what a vast difference there was between their reality
and the image so many young people had created of
them.

In that image many young people had blended their

personal needs, the need for protest, for vengeance, for justice at the family, professional and social levels; to the extent that they seemed to endanger an oppressive system they also seemed to guarantee the liberation of everyone. In reality, seen from close up, they were nothing of all this.

Three out of the five had undertaken university studies; one had done a fair amount of traveling, had spent some months in America, had run out of money there and had been bailed out by the embassy, and he recounted these experiences boastingly. What had they to do with what is called the proletariat? At the university they had completed no courses, abroad they had fun at the public's expense: with regard to the proletariat, did they, by any chance, belong to the enemy class? Once back in Italy they had promptly gone underground only to surface in the world of the nation's prisons. While grappling with these things it seemed to Cino that to dissolve this seductive influence that every terrorist organization had upon young people it would suffice to make them a little better known, to film one of their days, to tape their discussions, to show all and sundry what they were actually like: "Here they are!" It was not they themselves that were dangerous; it was their idealizations.

Those people having removed to "La Dolce Vita," three completely different prisoners arrived in Cino's cell: whereas the former bunch would have spent their whole lives in the struggle, these looked like they had surrendered even before they were born. They sat huddled together on the bench for hours on end, silent and empty, like vagrants. For days on end they slept the sleep of brute beasts, heavy and motionless, mouths open. When they were awake they almost never exchanged a word, they confined themselves to looking at one another as if they were unable to see. When they did talk they had cracked, somewhat squeaky voices, like bats, as if their vocal cords, for too long unused, had trouble finding the right vibration. Evident in all was a total lack of energy, as if not only their limbs, their muscles, but even their eyes, nose, larynx were incapable of fulfilling their function. Even though they were three, and the cell was pretty small, they left Cino with the impression he was alone. If one was lying on the floor he would step over him. If Cino asked a question no one would reply, at best one might turn his eyes toward Cino and produce a stupid smile, almost to apologize for not even having heard the question. There it was: these people had indeed stopped time: they lived in a world apart, where nothing ever happened: a sort of limbo. Joy perhaps did not exist there; but neither, one could suppose, did the least bit of pain.

Cino noticed that the moment when they livened up a little and sometimes squabbled was when mail came: were one of them to receive a letter, a package, a book, the others would be all over him, carefully observing the opening of the envelope, the unfolding of the sheets inside, the peeling off of the stamp: it seemed that every minute corner of every object could contain something precious. The precious thing that alone could unify their lives and rouse them for an instant every couple of days was heroin. In prison anyone who surrenders has an urgent need of it: with heroin to transform him he becomes as elusive as Proteus: prison, memories, crises, breakdown, he can be got to by none of these.

Someone who has taken heroin is not where he is: he is elsewhere. And in fact if in the cell it was cold they would sit about naked, as if they were on the equator; and if it

was hot all three would have a scarf around their necks as
if to protect their tonsils. Nothing could have affected
them: not a life sentence, not their mother's death, not
one of them collapsing. They were living in a private re-
gion, the geographical map of which was drawn by sores
upon the nose and infected veins in arms and feet. Wher-
ever they were, they could call themselves exiles.

They were—what is one to say?—incapable of any effort whatever. Even of laughing. Indeed one afternoon
one of the three started laughing all by himself, and at a
certain point the laughter turned into gagging, as if a foreign body were choking him. He puts his hand to his
mouth, extracts the body and looks: a tooth. Whereupon
the two others start tittering, quietly, with little twitches,
and while keeping this up they open their mouths and
with a finger point to where they are missing teeth: by
now they had less than half of their teeth, and those were
so loose as to seem just sitting there: a burst of laughter
was enough to spatter them around like shrapnel.

To live day and night with others who drug themselves
means to drug oneself day and night. It is like traveling on
a train in a compartment full of smokers: you yourself do
not smoke but when you get off the train you have
clogged lungs and a headache: the others have smoked
for you also, for an hour you have breathed the smoke
blown from their mouths and noses, you have it everywhere inside you, even your clothes are imbued with it, if
a doctor came up to you and smelled your breath he'd
say: "A smoker!" Thus, someone who were to glance into
Cino's cell of an afternoon around three, after the arrival
of the mail, and beholding all four of them sitting or
sprawling about without saying a word as if oblivious to
each other, would have concluded at once: "All junkies."

In reality, living together with them there it was impossible that in the long run Cino fail to pick up the habits, tics, manias and the apathy of the others.

His problem and their problem was the same: prison. They had found a solution. Cino was convinced it was wrong but he himself had no other. And, furthermore, he didn't exactly know what solution that one was.

And so one afternoon during which the others did not have problems but he did—they had postponed his trial for the third time—he straightened out a finger, poked it into the white powder, and sniffed.

It was not the only time. In that experience there is only the beginning, there is no end. When Cino discovered that heroin takes away pain and in exchange bestows an even greater anguish, it was by then too late: the absence of pain was really the absence of any sensation, as if an electric scalpel had severed the nerve bundles at their base: an anaesthetic destined to have unlimited effect until it produces permanent unconsciousness. Perhaps in this way Cino had escaped the woes of prison: but he had proceeded like someone who to eliminate the pain in a finger cuts off his arm.

At first Cino had had the problem of obsessive ideas, they would visit him in the afternoons, at night; now he no longer had that problem because he had no more ideas, he had no more brains. In a certain sense no one could have done him harm anymore, but anyone could have done what he wanted with him.

And so for the prosecution the trial had been as easy as you please: Cino did not even realize that he was supposed to defend himself, and since in the group of persons arrested more than one had actually been carrying a weapon, Cino ended up among those who received the heaviest sentences. Just before they led him away Sirio looked at him for a long moment, incredulous: this boy who didn't even know where he was, who moved his jaws all the time, scratched his eyebrow, who while they were pronouncing sentence upon him had bent over to tie his shoelace, this was not Cino: he wasn't anybody.

2: SELF-AWARENESS

Cino was substantially the last to fall in that lost battle. The battle had been lost up and down the whole line and this bound one to reconsider every phase of it. Everything had gone wrong, perhaps because everyone had been wrong. If that was so then it was a good thing it had been lost, for it would have been a graver misfortune still had it been won by men who were wrong.

A profound change had now come over the city: in schools they studied, in factories they worked, at concerts they paid to get in, radios played music uninterruptedly. Upon the public squares, in the evening, after the shops closed, discrete crowds converged, people went for a walk, showed themselves, conversed. Now and then, every two or three months, television and the press would report some terrorist attack, but it was always a minor piece of news, there was nothing more to explain or to understand: the few desperate groups of terrorists still ac-

118

tive resembled the leftovers after a war: once in a while something explodes but you don't call that a war. The war is over, everything seems to have gone back to the way it was before.

And yet going back to the way it was before is impossible. The young people have understood forever that that life has no meaning and refuse to accept it as it is proposed. Where they cannot create an alternative for themselves, instead of living in a mistaken world they go to live in a world apart, reserved and intangible: in drugs. Each young person who chooses drugs enters an abstract world as remote as the kingdom of the dead; and leaves our history.

The others, meanwhile, went on searching. They would gather in school classrooms, in university lecture halls, at the free radio stations. Almost all, and Sirio among them, had returned home to get their bearings once again. They organized meetings with French and German contemporaries to find out what others of their age were doing in other parts of the world. They met in bookstores, without a program, just to get together.

Thus Sirio too and Carla and others in their circle got in the habit of meeting in a students bookstore every evening after the closing hour, to discuss things to do for those in jail and things to do for themselves. Younger teenagers came also, who had not taken part in their struggles but knew of them through the press; and they did not want to repeat the same errors. They all installed themselves in a whitewashed room at the back of the store and did what they wanted. They smoked. They ate. They talked. They slept. They listened to the radio. Some stayed all night long, others went away when they felt like it.

For weeks and months nothing happened: it was only a way to be together, sometimes boring. Some quarrel would start, some friendship would end, some other would be founded. Then all of a sudden the group began to function as a *group*, to become an ensemble of people who come together and talk because they have the same problems and because a solution found by one may therefore have validity for all, and by looking for it together there is a greater likelihood of finding it.

This was their first discovery: they liked being together, boys and girls, without parents. Boys ought to live, grow, study and think together with girls; the separation of boys from girls is part of a system that separates employers and workers, that creates rich and poor.

In the group were a boy and a girl who had fallen in love with each other. They went to the same school but were in different classes. At the beginning of the school year they did not even know one another. Now, if they wished to be together, it was their right to be placed in the same classroom simply by requesting it. All that conduces to happiness is right. They would ask the principal, and should the principal refuse one could consider occupying the school. All agreed.

The second discovery they made was this: whatever any one person says, upon whatever subject, concerns all. If someone does not feel involved it is because he does not know that he is.

The third discovery was that they had advanced into enemy territory creating a void behind them: this was the error that had been their undoing. As if, when he advanced into Russia, Napoleon had burned down each town he came to. In this way they had sabotaged factories and occupied schools, paralyzing them: in one year they had missed up to three hundred classes apiece. Result: they were a crowd of ignoramuses. They knew less. And difference in respect to knowledge lies at the base of difference in respect to power. It would have been far more revolutionary, for example, instead of never going to school, to have gone to school twice as much; perhaps now the situation would be the reverse.

This had already been grasped by whomever it was who, seeing on the walls of that room these words written with a marking pen:

FIGHT THE ESTABLISHMENT SCHOOL

had corrected them, whenever that was, so that they read:

A SCHOOL THAT FIGHTS THE ESTABLISHMENT

To be rid of the establishment we have to create a new school, and attend it. So the school is to be changed in order that it function not *for* but *against*. But to destroy everything means to be left without anything. They were without anything.

There they were, huddled on the floor, at the back of the bookstore, looking for something to take possession of.

One evening a girl brought a can of red spray paint and proposed to write some things on the wall in front. Nobody had any objections. While they all sat there on the floor, some smoking, some drinking Coca-Cola, some reading a newspaper, this still unknown girl who had always come to those meetings but had never opened her mouth went up to the wall and with the red spray slowly wrote these words:

MY FAMILY LOVES ME
BUT WRONGS ME

Having finished the sentence the girl turned, placed the can on a table, and went back to huddle amidst her companions. All were looking at her. She was a smallish girl, very dark, slight and nervous, a bundle of nerves held together by a belt, but shy, with eyes that were always lowered. She was kneeling on the floor but after a minute during which all stared at her she leaned forward on her knees and straightened up and drew a little comb through her flowing hair. In so doing she raised her bent arms and her breasts lifted inside her blouse. She was wearing a white blouse buttoned in front up to the neck and with three-quarter sleeves ending with an open-work hem. It resembled the stole of a priestess. She is here to perform a rite, Sirio was saying to himself as he gazed at her, the rite of beauty. "What's your name?" asked the companion nearest to the girl. And she answered: "Marta."

The group was looking at the inscription without saying anything. In that silence the girl's story took shape in the minds of all. In Sirio's mind it was being formulated like this: Marta's family loved her, perhaps too much; it took care of her, kept an eye on her, wanted her to be like the others in the family, therefore did not let her live her life. So Marta had begun doing just what her mother did not want, to regain control of her life. As if getting up each morning Marta would ask herself: What does my mother not want? That's just what I shall do. Surely her mother did not want her to be here: that is why Marta was here. And she did not want Marta to write a sentence like that one: she wrote it for that reason.

While these thoughts were developing in Sirio's mind one of those present had risen, picked up the can and stationed himself before the wall. But he obviously did not have his ideas ready, for there he stood, holding the can, staring at the wall and not moving. Finally he gave up the

idea of composing something of his own; he took a step
and planted himself before what Marta had written and
with the spray sprayed a line through the word *but* and
above it wrote *therefore:* the sentence now read:

MY FAMILY LOVES ME
THEREFORE WRONGS ME

He turned about, placed the can on the table and went
back to huddle amidst the others, but this time next to
Marta: as if altering her sentence in that way had made
him her intimate friend.

The group sat there in its astonishment, with Marta
perhaps the most astonished of all. Each read and reread
the original sentence and then this one, and each wondered whether the first really contained the second. The
harm that her family was doing to Marta, did it really
come from the fact that it loved her? Love and self-inter-
est, love and sadism, are they then the same thing? Is
there then so much that is harmful in these middle class
families, permissive and protective, corrupted and cor-
rupting? What they have to teach, is it therefore nothing?
Ought even their love to be shunned? Each person in the
group looked at the sentence and looked at it again; no
one spoke; each realized that they must make no sound,
cause no disturbance lest they lose this opportunity to
seize hold of the truth that had never lain so close to
hand. Even those who were smoking were exhaling
slowly, gently, almost as if smoke too might make a
sound. Certainly in that room no sentence had ever been
pronounced that had such a compelling and such a lasting
effect within every nook and cranny of those young people's spirits.

Each now looked at the new sentence, lingered over
each word, tried and tried again to trim, to edit, to change,

to correct, in the conviction that other, as yet obscure
meanings were contained in those seemingly very trans-
parent words. No one felt inclined to write other sentences on other walls: all were convinced that their group
encounter was going to revolve entirely around Marta's
sentence alone. It was as though each were attempting to
use Marta's life as the starting point for an explanation of
his own. Marta had this particular relationship with her
family: her family loved her and yet, precisely on account
of this, without realizing, was doing her harm. What did
the relationship with his parents imply for each one of
those other young people? What did it reveal? What epi-
sodes, what traumas did it explain? All of them? Young
people who a moment before, had Marta not written that
sentence and had her companions not corrected it, would
have taken turns writing to protest against school, against
factory, against the price of movie or concert tickets,
against insufficient lunchrooms and public transport,
against the principal or against grades, those same young
people now found they had altogether forgotten whatever
it was they had been of a mind to write, and found themselves utterly absorbed by this discovery of the harm
contained in the mistaken love of their parents or, which
comes to the same thing, in the love of mistaken parents.
All were milling about, examining, excavating that sentence to see what else it contained, as when a group of
prospectors go looking for gold and one finds some and
then all run to where that one is and dig and scrabble
about and sift the same pebbles and sand.

Now the words written on the wall were these:

MY FAMILY
WRONGS ME

He who had crossed out all the other words had already sat down and disappeared into the middle of the group. Very likely near Marta, he too.

As one by one each discerned a new meaning in Marta's sentence—that is, in Marta's life, but therefore in his own as well, for no one can express a truth unless he has it within him—each also drew physically closer to her, as if to extend this community of feeling into a community of living: whispering to one another, touching one another, one lighting his cigarette from another's, but looking each other in the eye. Marta had a loose shoelace and now the friend was tying it for her.

Another girl now stood in front of the wall and she was holding the can to her stomach with both hands; her head was cocked to one side, she was thinking. Then she straightened her head and slowly crossed out all the words in the sentence save two:

FAMILY
WRONGS

All shook their heads, some smiled, as if the new discovery had been too easy. But that's what happens with all discoveries, the scientific and even the geographic: from a first discovery, perhaps casual, many others follow, one easier than the last. But if the first had not been made these final ones, so elementary, would not have been even thinkable.

Family and harm, then, are the same thing. The whole group had said it. The problem for children is above all the relationship to their parents. To bring about a revolution means, at bottom, to do the contrary of what your parents want. And this is inevitable, when your parents are wrong. Or, to put it better, when this is inevitable it means that your parents are wrong. But if the family is harmful as well, what is left? Is evil everywhere? And in fact the last boy had crossed out one more word and a letter of the remaining one, leaving only this:

WRONG

All is wrong and therefore one must say no to everything. And redo everything. Be new fathers. New mothers. Create new children, never yet seen. Love them differently. From the world such as it is nothing useful can come to you. All that you receive will end up harming you, and sooner or later you will pay for it. Your family especially. Once you have discovered this, you have discovered that everything is wrong; and now you're in for it.

It was doubtless because of this that Marta was crying. In her little corner, still huddled up on the floor (half the group had got up by now) with her face pressed against her knees, she was weeping submissively. Now and then she seemed to shiver. The group had narrowed around her, by this time they were all on their feet and someone was trying to help her up also. But only when her crying had subsided did Marta lift her still tear-streaked face and raise her arms to either side to be taken and pulled up. Once she was on her feet a girl who had had a hand in transforming her sentence came up and kissed her, holding her tight for some time.

The main reason why young people feel good together is not because they have the same problems but because they are the same age. The young will more easily join one another in committing a crime than perform a good deed along with someone of a different age. And so you are much more likely to find a boy from Autonomia* and a boy from Comunione e Liberazione** in each other's company than an adult communist and a Catholic. As a matter of fact, in that group which gathered in the back of the bookstore there was one lad from Comunione e Liberazione.

That evening, since some of the others were hauling out the problems they had, he decided to spell out the truth about himself: he got up, went to the wall and wrote:

MY PROBLEM IS GOD

He headed back to where he had been sitting, not looking at anybody's face. He was expecting a hostile reaction, one of disapproval, or at least a sneer; young people are cruel. Nothing happened: by now they had created an atmosphere so favorable to understanding and analysis as to exclude censure: to every new statement each responded by simply asking himself what it meant.

The appearing of that sentence upon the wall, a sentence so unlike the earlier one, produced a strange effect: here, obviously, was someone different from the others but while five years ago he would have been chucked out bodily, now he was looked at with curiosity, as if he had in his possession something the others did not and for which they too might have a need. Five years earlier the pressure of the Movement upon the whole city had been so strong as to shut young Christians up in their centers as in new catacombs; now that pressure had fallen to zero, and the Christians were flowing out in every direction

* Left-wing political formation. (Tr. note.)
** Catholic political formation. (Tr. note.)

and lo! something of theirs, a droplet, had arrived here. It was a fact to take note of.

Everyone was looking at him, saying nothing, seeking the point of contact to set the conversation going.

"Mankind is divided into two parts," someone began, "the part that believes and the part that doesn't. The two parts share nothing in common: in the course of a non-believer's day there is not a single minute that can be inserted in the day of a believer. And vice versa."

"Perhaps it isn't even that way," suggested someone else, "perhaps there's the half of mankind that believes but fears that there isn't anything, and the other half that does not believe but fears that it is all there."

"The problem is not of believing or not believing but of changing the world," said another companion. Others around him nodded in approval.

"In this," the boy from C. and L. put in, "there is something that unites us. We too want the liberation of the world but we believe that liberation will come not from an idea but from a person. That is why our criticisms are not directed just at you but at all the earth's ideologies. While in fact each of us in this world is committed to various activities and oriented in various directions, Christians are expected to uphold that the only salvation comes from one person."

A total silence followed that declaration. The twenty-odd companions gathered there had the feeling that a traveler has when after five minutes of exchanging glances and smiles with a fellow passenger on the train, he imagines he is going to be able to have a conversation with him only to hear his first question answered by a foreigner speaking in an unknown tongue.

"We meet here to find out what we have in common.

You wouldn't have come here in order to say you have nothing in common with us."

"We also meet together, we have meetings whose purpose is to help us become aware of ourselves and of the world and of our relationships with the world. We realized that we don't really know you at all, that you don't know us and that until now our relationships have had no meaning. I am here in order that they may acquire a meaning. And I ask you whether you will allow me to come back again when I want to."

This request left them all at a loss: it was not necessary, anyone was at liberty to come there and listen or speak whenever he chose. But that boy wanted to be accepted ahead of time, almost guaranteed admission, as if to an official meeting or a sort of debate.

Sirio suddenly remembered the time years before when the column of strikers marching toward the factories had passed in front of C. and L. headquarters and a group of students had gone inside to take it over and wreck it. And he had the impression now of a turnabout: expanding and marching upon the city, C. and L. was passing their way and a tiny detachment from that group of militants had entered their room with a view to bettering things there. It was the same battle, with different weapons. One had to accept it.

"Come whenever you like," he answered.

All assented. And to show him that his coming had not been pointless they went back to analyzing the sentence he had written on the wall. Singly or two at a time and in rapid succession several members of the group went up to what the Catholic boy had put on the wall, and his confession underwent alterations that modified it profoundly, finally altogether revolutionized it.

MY PROBLEM IS I

MY PROBLEM IS THAT I AM NOT

THE PROBLEM IS THAT THERE IS NO I

If God is and I know it, I am God, I can go through the fire singing. If the fire frightens me, if life daunts me, I am not God, and God is not in me. And mine cannot be called life: I am not. Thus it is with all of us: there is no I, I open the I and I do not find Me: inside are the Others.

In the place belonging to the I, first, foremost and within the I, there are the Others, in the shape of rules. This was the culminating point of the inquiry, the gleam of light at the end of the tunnel, the all-encompassing definition which communicates to you: *Thou art this.* This the boy and the girl had grasped, who in the remaining corner of the martyred wall had written something extreme, a sentence no one dared touch:

SERVITUDE IS NOTHING

NOTHING OTHER THAN

AN ORDER INSIDE YOURSELF

Sirio now glanced first at Marta, surrounded by a whole group of friends who were consoling her, then at his other companions who had participated in the analysis of those sentences. And that is when he understood two things. The first was that there, in that group, with those companions, he had glimpsed a new task, a new definition of life, very unlike that which had guided his earlier years in his family and unlike that in whose name he had struggled against the factory, and unlike the one which lay at the base of his love for Carla. The first was self-centered, the second destructive, the third private. This definition of life could perhaps be called critical, and this meaning of life expressed thus: we must remake ourselves; the greatest contribution to the liberation of others is the liberating of ourselves: we have discussed everything over and over again, with the exception of ourselves: let's discuss ourselves. To bring on a revolution is easy; the difficult part is to be revolutionaries.

The second thing Sirio understood was this: they had met many times there, together, in those sessions; there was so much to analyze, to understand, to transform: practically everything. One had to set up a great many Revolutionary Consciousness Groups, where each finally came into contact with others without losing but finding himself. From that Revolutionary Consciousness would derive a transforming influence that would radiate in all directions, affecting the couple, the family, school, office, factory, society. There had begun a revolution whose end he could not see: there is never any revolution if there is not above all a revolution within.

The design of this book is the work of
Austryn Wainhouse, of Marlboro, Vermont.
It was composed by
American-Stratford Graphic Services, Inc.,
of Brattleboro, Vermont.
The printing and binding were by
McNaughton & Gunn, Inc.,
of Ann Arbor, Michigan.